DONATED TO THE
THE VINEYARD SCHOOL

From

Olivia and Caroline Heyworth

Date

July 1995

MAN IN MOTION

J A N   M A R K

Illustrated by
Jeff Cummins

VIKING KESTREL

VIKING KESTREL
Published by the Penguin Group
27 Wrights Lane, London W8 5TZ, England
Viking Penguin Inc., 40 West 23rd Street, New York, New York 10010, USA
Penguin Books Australia Ltd, Ringwood, Victoria, Australia
Penguin Books Canada Ltd, 2801 John Street, Markham, Ontario, Canada L3R 1B4
Penguin Books (NZ) Ltd, 182–190 Wairau Road, Auckland 10, New Zealand

Penguin Books Ltd, Registered Offices: Harmondsworth, Middlesex, England

First published 1989
1 3 5 7 9 10 8 6 4 2

Text copyright © Jan Mark, 1989
Illustrations copyright © Jeff Cummins, 1989

Filmset in 12/14 pt Rockwell Light
Printed and bound in Great Britain by
Richard Clay Ltd, Bungay, Suffolk

A CIP catalogue record for this book is available from the British Library

ISBN 0–670–82670–7

To Murray and Gina

'Hello,' Lloyd said; 'am I speaking to Mr Stephen Sutton?'

'Lord Sutton to you. Who's that?' Stephen's voice, through the static on the line, sounded like someone speaking from the bottom of a bag of crisps.

'It's me, isn't it?' Had his own voice changed so much in three weeks? Perhaps it was at last beginning to break.

'Which me?'

'Lloyd, you bozo. We just got our phone connected.'

'Did you ring me up to celebrate? Jolly decent, old bean. What's it like?'

'The phone? Well, it's made of plastic, and it's green – same colour as your loo, Stephen –'

'Cut it out. I meant the new place.'

'It's OK,' Lloyd said.

'What about school?'

'We don't start till tomorrow, here.'

'What! We went back last week.'

'I know,' Lloyd said, and felt suddenly forlorn. The year planner, which he could see from where he stood, was stuck to the side of the fridge with magnets and still bore the dates of his old school terms. Things were different here. 'We went up there on Friday and had a look round. It's big; eight hundred and twenty students. The playing fields are huge.'

Now Stephen sounded forlorn. 'Is there a sports hall?'

'No, but there's two gymnasiums and cricket nets. We got this prospectus when we were there –'

'What's a prospectus?'

'It's that sort of magazine they give out about

1

how wonderful the school is and how many A levels they got last year, you know the sort of thing. It's probably lies, half of it, but it says lessons end early on Wednesdays and then you can choose what you do for the rest of the afternoon.'

'Like go home?' Stephen said.

'No, activities, you know, photography or frog-watching; but it's sport, mainly – badminton, basket ball . . .'

'Cricket?'

'Not this term, but it ought to be good. Mr Soames, he's head of PE, used to play for Derbyshire.'

'Soames? When?'

'During the war, by the look of him.'

'Name doesn't ring any bells.'

'Well, he *did*. And Mr Moran, the one who showed us around, he's a sort of deputy Soames, he –'

'Moron, did you say?'

'Mor*an*, you dipstick.'

'I bet they call him Moron. This line's terrible. You sure you got it plugged in right?'

'It's your end, not ours. Your phone's always on the blink. Ingrid had to ring New York this morning. She said the line was clearer than the speaking clock.'

'Did you watch the Giants last night?'

'The who?'

'The New York Giants, cretin.'

'Pygmies,' Lloyd said. 'You know I follow the Dolphins.'

'That's only because you're a conservation freak. Only nut I know who follows a team because he likes the helmets.'

'I'm working on Ingrid to get a video recorder – for the Super Bowl.'

'Won't she let you stay up for that?'

'Not till two in the morning.'

'You did this year.'

'That was only because she didn't know. She had to go to London overnight. She thought Barbara was sending me to bed at the right time, but she'd gone to this disco in Southampton and never got back till nearly four. She bribed me. If I didn't grass on her she wouldn't grass on me. I never thought she'd keep quiet, you know, she'd let it out by accident. She's got such a big mouth –'

'Do they play American football in Canada?'

'I think so.'

'My uncle's going over there in November. He might bring me back some gear.'

'You'll be lucky,' Lloyd said, his stomach growling with envy. His father was in Canada, and no gear was crossing the Atlantic in Lloyd's direction. 'It costs two hundred and fifty thousand dollars to equip a squad for a season.'

'But I'm not a squad,' Stephen said, reasonably. 'I'm getting a ball for my birthday.'

'Practice ball?'

'No, a real Wilson. We can take it down the rec.'

'No, we can't. You forgotten where I am?'

There was a pause at the other end of the line. Stephen *had* forgotten where Lloyd was, and for a moment Lloyd had been on the verge of forgetting, too.

'You could come over at half term,' Stephen said. It was a tempting thought, back among the old crowd again, knowing where he was and who he was.

'When's your half term – no, hang on.' He walked to the fullest extent of the telephone flex and looked at the year planner on the fridge. 'It's the twenty-second of October.'

'When's yours?'

'I don't know. It's probably in the prospectus.'

'Go and look, then.'

'I don't know where I put it. Everything's in such a mess here. We're decorating and half the stuff's still packed. Look, I'll find out tomorrow, won't I? Well, by the end of the week, anyway. I'll have to go. I just heard someone come in.'

'Aren't you meant to use the phone any more?'

'Yes, but it's long-distance now, remember, and Ingrid made me swear a solemn oath that I wouldn't ring till after six – cheap rate.'

'What did you swear?' Stephen sounded interested. He and Lloyd had been forming secret societies and swearing solemn oaths since they first met up at middle school.

'She made me swear on my mother's grave.'

'But she *is* your mother.'

'She wouldn't let a little thing like that bother her. I'll ring at the end of the week –'

'It's cheap rate all over the weekend.'

'OK, on Saturday. See you.'

'One fine day,' Stephen said.

CHAPTER ONE

Lloyd spent most of his first morning at North End Upper School at a table with a group of people who had all come up together from the same middle school. The day so far had been mainly occupied with administration, which meant that the class tutor made lists and filled in forms while the class chatted quietly or read books. No one at the table took much notice of Lloyd except for two pretty Asian girls, Farida and Farzana, who looked so alike that they might have been twins. When Lloyd smiled hopefully at them they smiled back; emboldened by this he spoke to them, but they still only smiled and spoke to no one but each other.

Toward lunch-time he found himself eavesdropping on two fellows at the table in front, Salman and Kenneth, who were compiling a kind of year book. Lloyd thought it a little premature to begin an enterprise like this on the first day of term, until he realized that they were making predictions about who, on present showing, was likely to be the brightest, thickest, most successful, least athletic, and so on. Salman was particularly ruthless in his forecasts and Lloyd listened with escalating anxiety as they debated The Man Most Likely to Succeed, The Man Least Likely to Change, and The Man Most Likely to Self-destruct, in case any of them should turn out to be him. He need not have worried; they were all Anwar Saddiq.

It seemed that neither Salman nor Kenneth had met Anwar before, but he was clearly the kind of person everyone remembers at once; not far off six feet tall and looking as if he would need to shave again before tea-time, he was head, shoulders and moustache above the rest of the class.

'How old?' Kenneth muttered.

'Twenty-five?' Salman replied, bitterly. Lloyd knew that even if Anwar's birthday fell at the very beginning of the school year he could not be more than fourteen and one week, but regardless of whether he was likely to succeed or self-destruct, he was definitely a man. His voice had broken, too.

Woman Most Likely to Make Waves had started off as one Katherine Kellett, nominated by Kenneth – Salman, Lloyd noticed, was not much concerned with the girls – and who had been at the middle school with them. The class had come together not two hours ago, but when they assembled after the official welcome from the head of year, Katherine had managed to collar a seat on the same table as Anwar Saddiq, and her hair, which had arrived at school in a prim knot, was dangling lustrously over her shoulder. But just as Salman and Kenneth began summing up, a late comer walked in, Zoe De La Hoyde. Her arrival was greeted with stunned silence, broken only by the reflective rasp of Anwar's thumb, browsing in his stubble. It was then that Kenneth revised the list, designating Zoe as Woman Most Likely to Make Waves, and Katherine as Woman Most Likely to Cause Trouble. Anwar was pruned succinctly to The Man Most Likely.

When they were dismissed to the canteen Lloyd began to wonder where he might sit and with whom. The school's intake was from five different middle schools, whose old comrades had stuck together so exclusively this morning, but it was clear that already new allegiances were forming. People were sitting down to eat with friends made during the last half hour. Lloyd took his tray from the serving hatch, smiled – but no more – at Farida and Farzana, and decided to risk joining Salman and Kenneth. There were three or four others at the table but they departed soon after he sat down, leaving just three of them and Katherine Kellett, who smouldered in silence.

Salman looked at him thoughtfully and said, 'Why did you come and sit with us?'

Lloyd flushed and started to stand up again. 'If that's how you feel –'

'I didn't mean it like that,' Salman said. 'It's just that we don't know you –'

'Shuddup, Iqbal!' Kenneth said, strangling Salman with an arm that shot out like a striking cobra. 'You can't take him anywhere,' he complained to Lloyd. 'What he means is, did you join us because of our irresistible magnetism, or because there wasn't room anywhere else?'

'There wasn't room,' Lloyd said, entering into the spirit of the thing. 'And I'm in your class. I sat at the back.'

'Out of respect?' Salman said.

'Don't take any notice of him, he's just trying to make you feel at home. He only insults his friends. When he starts being polite it's time to head for the fall-out shelter,' Kenneth said. 'Name, rank, number?'

'Lloyd Slater.'

'Not the Stamford Road Slaters from over the chip shop!' Salman cried. 'One of *them*? Aaaargh!'

'One of these days you are going to become seriously dead,' Kenneth said. 'Suppose he *is* one of the Stamford Road Slaters?'

'I live in Sackville Street,' Lloyd said.

'Not in our catchment area,' Kenneth said, knowledgeably. 'You must have appealed to get in here.'

'He *is* appealing, isn't he?' Salman said, examining Lloyd with his head on one side.

'Shut *up*, Iqbal,' Kenneth said. 'You weren't by any chance at school with The Man Most Likely, were you?' He pointed across the canteen to where Anwar was holding court at a crowded table.

'Him? No, we've only been there a month – only just moved here anyway. We're from Hampshire.'

'Gosh. Foreigners,' Salman said.

'My mother inherited the house. It was my great-aunt's and Ingrid – my mother – grew up near here so she thought she might as well come back.'

'Didn't you mind changing schools?' Kenneth said, 'leaving all your mates and that?'

'I was changing schools anyway, wasn't I?' Lloyd said. He didn't say anything about missing his friends and the others, to his relief, did not pursue the matter. 'Keep an eye on the time,' he said. 'They don't have bells here.'

'That's to make us self-reliant, I expect,' Salman said, poker-faced. 'You heard what they said at that meeting this morning, we can't expect nursemaids here. We've got to learn to organize ourselves. What is a nursemaid, Lin?'

'Search me,' Kenneth said. 'I never had one. Let's get organized, you guys. What have we got next?'

'CDT. We all in the same group for CDT?'

They gathered up their lunch boxes and headed for the door. Lloyd, who was not in their group for CDT, returned his tray to the hatch and lingered to see if Katherine Kellett was going in his direction, but she left by a circuitous route that took her past the table of The Man Most Likely. Lloyd went off on his own.

They all met up again in the drive at the end of the afternoon. Kenneth and Salman had bicycles and had collected another old lag from their last school, a boy who carried two badminton racquets and balanced his school bag on Salman's saddle. When Lloyd asked him, he said his name was Vlad the Impaler, which might have been true. He had a pallid, bloodsucking look and long eye-teeth.

'Haven't you got a bike?' Kenneth said, 'or do you walk for the exercise?'

'I'll bring it tomorrow,' Lloyd said. 'I wanted to see what the parking arrangements were like, first.'

'Make sure you've got a good lock,' Kenneth said. 'My brother left here last year. He warned me. And never leave your pump on the bike.'

Salman and Vlad the Impaler were in front, exchanging jokes picked up in the holidays.

'I've heard that one before,' Salman was saying. 'Now I'll tell you a story, a really horrible story ...' he leered back at them over his shoulder, '. . . about the England Selectors . . .'

'He's been absolutely unbearable since Pakistan won the Test,' Kenneth said. 'Mind you, he's always been pretty hard going.'

'You known him a long while?'

'Oh, we go way back,' Kenneth said, hinting at decades of close involvement. 'Middle school, first school, maternity ward . . .'

'Really?'

'Not quite. He was born in Bedford, but it was the same week as me. If he'd lived here then we'd probably have met at birth.'

Salman was far ahead of them now, cycling on the pavement and chanting in a wild high voice, 'Gower ... Gatting ... Gooch ... Gooooch ... Gooooooooooooch.'

'Has he always been like this?' Lloyd said.

'A nutter, you mean?' said Vlad, who had been left behind. 'Oh yes, but it's worse in summer.'

'The heat?'

'The cricket.'

Salman ran his bicycle into a black plastic rubbish bag left on a corner for the dustmen to collect, and waited for them to catch up. Kenneth coasted up to him from behind and clouted him round the head. 'Sober up, Iqbal, the season's over.'

'Hooligan time,' Salman said, disgustedly. 'Nine

months of mud and skinheads. Go boil your boots.' He reversed the bicycle out of the rubbish bag and punched Kenneth in the neck by way of farewell. Vlad was standing on the corner waving the badminton racquets like a man directing a taxiing aircraft and Kenneth cycled precariously round him, arms spread, like a taxiing aircraft, before turning off down a side street.

'See you tomorrow,' he called. Lloyd, left alone again, watched him go. Salman clamped his fingers round the handlegrips, stood on his pedals and steered into the roadway. Vlad the Impaler, a badminton racquet rammed up each sleeve, perched on the saddle and made paddling motions with the racquets.

'See you, then,' Lloyd called after them. Neither head turned, but four legs waved him a cheerful goodbye as Vlad rowed them decorously out of sight.

Home was also round the corner, but it was a different corner, further down the road. In the month that Lloyd had been living in Sackville Street he had been experimenting with different routes home, convinced, like the men who set out to discover the North-West Passage, that one of them would eventually turn out to be a short cut.

The month had been taken up with settling in and decorating, and most of Lloyd's excursions had been in search of Post Offices, chemists or a shop that would sell Polyfilla at nine o'clock in the evening. It was only on Friday, visiting the school for the first time, that they had discovered Stamford Road which was the high street for the suburb of North End. The shops in Stamford Road sold everything, at all hours; you could even, he'd discovered, buy a four-poster bed in Stamford

Road, although not after five-thirty. All the turnings on the east side led into the interconnecting streets of the triangular enclave that was North End. He knew which street he lived in, he could even pin-point it on a map, but it was still a welcome surprise to find himself going in the right direction, turning on the right corner, recognizing a shop or a pillar box.

Home, near the far end of Sackville Street, was a grey brick detached house, taller than the terraces on either side and wider, as though it had got there first and stuck out its elbows, to make sure that it had plenty of room when the others began to crowd in. One steep gable, like a raised eyebrow, gave it a supercilious look. 'We got *class*,' it seemed to be saying. This might have been the case, once, for the original owners had given it a name, Oxenford Lodge, which Ingrid refused to use, in spite of Barbara's pleading.

'How can you boast about living at Oxenford Lodge and then bring people home to this dump?' Ingrid demanded.

'Oh, I wouldn't use it with the kind of people I bring home,' Barbara had said. 'I'd just keep it for boasting. Go on, Mummydearest, put it on the letter-head.'

'We are not having a letter-head,' Ingrid said.

'Go on. It'd be a good larf.' Barbara could turn anything into a good laugh, even having no father. 'It's a good larf,' she said, when people sympathized. Lloyd did not think it was so funny. His sister was a rock-bottom poser. She signed her letters *Barbara Ingridsdottir*, which she said was the Icelandic way, although Ingrid's family had come from Sweden, not Iceland. Ingrid was a translator; however, the languages she translated were neither Swedish nor Icelandic, but Hungarian and Finnish. Unlike Barbara she was a realist, and Lloyd wished she could have been less of a realist when describing their house as a dump. Auntie Karin had rented it as bedsits, and now they were trying to turn it back into a nice place to live; calling it a dump suggested that she had given up believing that they would ever succeed.

The Mummydearest business was a pose, too. Barbara called her that only when she was looking for a fight.

Ingrid was at work when he let himself in. He could hear the typewriter clattering upstairs, accompanied by a grinding squeak which was the leg of Ingrid's desk working up and down on a loose floorboard. The hall smelled sourly of fresh paint and there were letters on the doormat. Lloyd instantly deduced that his mother had been decorating this morning but had gone upstairs to work before the second post was delivered. He was appalled. The post came at ten; she must have been up there ever since, not even coming down for lunch, not even for coffee, in the big front bedroom which had become her study; translating. When he was small he thought that *translating* was the word for typing, since the two usually went together.

He called up the stairs: 'D'you want a coffee?'

The clattering halted. 'Is that Barbara?'

Lloyd was affronted for a moment, but admitted that she must find it difficult to identify a voice with that racket going on. The typewriter was an old Olivetti, built like a tank and with a motor that sounded like a corporation dustcart grinding

13

refuse. 'Ten years without a service,' Ingrid would boast sometimes, slapping it proudly. '*And* it was second-hand when I got it.' When the end came it would be loud and terrible; D-Day, Armageddon, Celtic v. Rangers.

He climbed to the bend in the stairs. 'No, it's me.'

'Already?'

'It's gone four.'

'How was school?'

'O K,' Lloyd said, guardedly.

'Bring up the coffee and we'll talk.'

He dumped his bag and went down again, taking care to avoid any paint that might still be damp and inflict pink blushes on his black sweater. The kitchen was at least completed, Ingrid had insisted on that. 'I can sleep on a clothesline,' she had said when Barbara proposed that they decorate the bedrooms first, 'and I can bath in a bucket, but I won't cook over a candle.'

The three of them had made a good job of it, he thought; it still looked like a kitchen in a catalogue – even the stove was clean – but someone had spoiled the picture by leaving an empty milk bottle and an empty coffee jar on the draining board; also an empty bag that had held sliced bread.

The Barbarian horde, Lloyd said to himself. His sister had had friends in. How had she managed to make so many so fast? There were five unwashed mugs in the sink. She would be back at university soon, she didn't even have a school to make friends in. Lloyd had the school, the friends were all left behind in Hampshire.

He returned to the bend in the stairs and called, 'We're out of coffee. Shall I go and get some?'

When Lloyd and Barbara were younger they had been taught that when Ingrid was in her study she was out at work and not to be disturbed. No one bothered about that any more, since they were past the age when they would hover about fiddling with things and blathering, although Lloyd had his doubts about Barbara, but the habit was hard to break.

'Come in, don't stand there yelling,' Ingrid called back, unreasonably. Lloyd went on up and opened the door of the front bedroom. In spite of being twice the size of her last study it was just as crowded; desk, table, filing cabinet, overflowing bookcases and tottering columns of books.

'Did you say something about coffins?' Ingrid asked. Lloyd located her among the book stacks by a rising thread of smoke.

'The whole lot'll go up in flames one of these days,' he said gloomily.

'You've been saying that for years.'

'You haven't given up yet.'

'I've given up eleven times,' Ingrid said, grinding out her cigarette. 'What's all this with the coffins?'

'*Coffee*. Barbara used it all up. Who did she have in?'

'The Dyno-rod Ladies Rugby Fifteen, by the sound of it.' Ingrid foraged for money in the drawer of her desk. 'Can you go up to the Co-op? Get a big jar this time.'

'That's what I said.'

'When?'

'On the landing, when you thought I was talking about coffins. How does she know so many people? We've only been here a month.'

'Some people attract other people. Like wasps round jam jars.'

'Like flies round –'

'Did *you* make any friends today?'

'Give us a chance,' Lloyd said, but he knew that after one day at a new school Barbara would have made friends. It was not that he himself found it difficult to make them, but the move, the sudden separation from the friends that he had known all his life, had been like a blade coming down, like a portable guillotine that gave you on one side a whole sheet of paper the size you wanted, on the other, a discarded strip that fell away. Lloyd felt like that discarded strip. How long before he could remake himself whole, become Lloyd Slater again and not an anonymous stranger who was asked, 'Why did you sit with us?'

He was sorry that it had been Salman Iqbal who had done the asking. He had sat at that table because, having observed Salman and Kenneth in class he had thought, as Barbara would have said, that they looked like a good laugh.

'We could always have tea.'

'Eh?'

'If you don't feel like going for coffee right away.'

He realized that he was still standing by Ingrid's desk, holding the money.

'No, I'll go. It won't take a minute by bike.' He would not ride the bicycle to school until he'd got a shackle lock, but the Co-op had plate glass windows. He would be able to keep an eye open for bicycle thieves.

The Co-op, not the big one in the city but a small local branch, was full of little children. Lloyd, tying his bicycle to the bus stop with a useful length of coaxial cable that would delay any thief long enough for Lloyd to rush out and apprehend him, saw them swarming in at the door and thought they were raiding the joint. He edged in at the tail end, half expecting that at any moment they would all come streaming out again, pursued by a furious assistant, but when he was inside he saw that they were all lined up, quiet and polite, behind an elder boy who was filling a wire basket with packets of crisps. He carried a cricket bat. It was Salman.

'They all yours?' Lloyd said, as Salman turned and recognized him.

'They're all *with* me,' Salman said. 'The Aston Road Under Eleven Eleven, give or take a few.'

'I thought they were your brothers and sisters.'

'Just a few of them,' Salman said, pointing randomly. 'Sadaf and Humayun. They don't all play,' he explained, 'the crisps are to keep the rest quiet.' Humayun looked like Salman, only half his height, but just as sharp.

Lloyd picked out the largest jar of coffee he could find. 'Where do you play?'

'Victoria Park, it's at the end of our road. Very convenient. Do you want to come along?'

Lloyd flourished his coffee. 'I can't, yet. Ingrid's waiting at home. I could come later.'

'We'll be there for hours,' Salman said. 'Come when you're ready. It'll be nice to have a few more my size.' They moved to the checkout.

'You won't ask me why I've come, if I do?' Lloyd said.

'Oh . . . lunch-time.' Salman tried to look apologetic. 'I don't *mean* to be rude,' he said sorrowfully, 'I just *am*. See you later.'

Lloyd left him rounding up his cricket team,

remembering that he had forgotten to look out for the bicycle, but it was still where he had left it, tethered to the bus stop like a patient dog.

When he reached home the telephone was ringing. He raced through the kitchen to the hall, where it hung on the wall, but before he could lay hands on it the ringing stopped. Ingrid, in the study, had got to the extension first. After a moment he heard a door open upstairs and his mother's voice called down, 'Are you back?'

'No.'

'Pity, it's for you.'

'That you?' Stephen said.

'No, who's that?'

'Knock knock.'

'Who's there?'

'Toodle.'

'Toodle Who?'

'Don't say that, I've only just got here. Boom boom!'

'I was going to ring you on Saturday, wasn't I?'

'Wanted to know what your school's like.'

'O K, I think. Hard to tell. Big.'

'You found out about half term, yet?'

'Give us a chance,' Lloyd said. 'I've only been there one day. We spent most of the time finding out what groups we're in.'

'Anybody duff you up?'

'Tried to. There's this mob in the Fourth Year, think they're hard. They hang around the lockers and stick their feet out as you go past. Then when you fall over they accuse you of kicking them and kick you back.'

'Did you get kicked?'

'No, I mean, this lot, they're so thick. I mean, it doesn't work unless they take you by surprise. After a couple of times we could all see what they were up to. This guy who tried it on me, when he stuck his leg out I just picked it up and he fell over.'

'Picked up his *leg*?'

'He had these baggy trousers on so I grabbed the slack and just kept lifting. It was lunch-time. He was eating yoghurt.'

'Did he spill it?'

'It went all over the boy next to him. I just kept walking. When I looked round they were beating each other up.'

19

'What are the teachers like?'

'Class Tutor's nice, Mrs Stone, but she's pregnant. I reckon we shall lose her before Christmas. You were right about Moron, he's our Year Tutor, but he's OK. I don't know about the others, all they did was give us books to read while they made lists. All the groups are the wrong size; only four of us turned up for geography and there were thirty-nine in CDT. They were like bartering us, you know? "I'll take six of yours if you'll have Wallace," so we all started wondering what was wrong with Wallace.'

'What was?'

'I don't know, he never showed up, did he? That may have been the trouble, sort of like a bit left over when you've finished a jigsaw puzzle. He's supposed to be in my group for Latin, so I'll meet him if he ever gets here.'

'You're doing *Latin*? What for?'

'It was either that or German,' Lloyd said. 'I thought it'd make a change. This boy I'm playing cricket with, Salman, he's doing Latin too. He says it'll be a piece of cake after Arabic.'

'Why's he do Arabic?'

'He's learning the Koran by heart, he told me. He says he talks Urdu at home and English at school *and* he does French – well, we all do French.'

'Frizzo broke his arm,' Stephen said.

'Fighting?'

'No, the assault course.'

The assault course was in an overgrown chalk pit. From small beginnings, a broken ladder propped against a tree, it had developed into a death-trap adventure playground, causing the kind of injuries you lied about when you got home.

Lloyd thought of it wistfully. Had he not been *here*, he would have been *there*, at this very moment probably, swinging from tree to tree, breaking his own arm perhaps, and all his mates would call round to cheer him up.

'I'll give him a ring, later.'

There was an indistinct quacking on the line.

'You got company?'

'Dad, yelling about the phone bill. You'd better call me, next time.'

'I was going to, wasn't I? Only you couldn't wait.'

Far away Stephen hung up and the line went dead.

CHAPTER TWO

'What did Stephen want?'
Ingrid asked, as Lloyd
carried the coffee mugs
into the study.

'Just to see how I got on at school. Did you
know there's a man on the roof?'

'I had noticed.'

'I saw him when I came in. Who is he?'

'A cowboy. He arrived in an unmarked van.'

'What are you on about?' Lloyd said. The
cowboy could be heard scrabbling, far above
them. The sound travelled down the chimney
which Ingrid had blocked against draughts with a
bin liner stuffed full of screwed-up paper. 'Is he
doing the slates?'

'I hope so. He knocked on the door just after
you went out and said he was working up the
road and noticed two of our slates were missing.
Would I like him to replace them?'

'Is that what he's doing now?'

'Sounds like it.'

'How long does it take to put slates in?'

'Ah, but when he got up there he found the flashing round the chimney was damaged so he's fixing that, meanwhile putting his foot through a few more slates, no doubt. Still, the roof did need mending.'

'I bet *you're* being done.'

'Probably. But he's still cheap.'

'Shall I go up and see what he's doing?'

'It doesn't matter,' Ingrid said. 'I'm sure we can afford not to have a leaky roof. The chimney needs repointing – that'll have to wait.'

'Why don't we have a lodger?' Lloyd said.

'Instead of a chimney?'

'No, instead of you working such long hours. We could put him in the attic.'

'Him?'

Lloyd paused. 'Or her.'

'But preferably him?' Ingrid lit a cigarette guiltily, took one drag under Lloyd's accusing stare, and ground it out again. The cowboy on the roof dropped something and they heard it slithering down the slates. 'You're fed up with living in a house full of women?'

'Not really,' Lloyd said. 'I'm more fed up with living in a house full of Barbara. Look, you'd have more money if you didn't smoke, wouldn't you?'

'Barbara will be gone quite soon. I know how you feel, I spent my formative years in a house full of men.'

'You had Gran.'

'We were outnumbered five to two. Your uncles grew up thinking that women were an oppressed minority.'

'I thought they *were* oppressed.'

'But hardly a minority,' Ingrid said. 'Are you home for good, now?'

'Do you mind if I go and play cricket for a bit?'

'Aye aye, a social life at last,' Ingrid said. 'Who with?'

'This boy from school, Salman. I met him in the Co-op.'

'Salman? Is that his Christian name?'

'Not Christian,' Lloyd said. 'He's a Muslim – well, I should think he is. Salman Iqbal. He's a bit of a loony, too.'

'Cricketers are. Just the two of you – playing, I mean?'

'Oh no, he's got all these little kids as well, to play with. They were all in the shop with him, being good and doing what he told them. Do you know where my bat is?'

'Sorry, it'll be in one of the tea-chests in the attic, but I'd rather you didn't go fossicking around up there just yet. You might get the glass-ware by mistake.'

'I expect Salman'll lend his. Are you going to stop work yet?'

'Soon. I promised myself two more pages.'

Lloyd went out by the back door, over the uneven pavement that was being gradually invaded by the lawn. The lawn itself was four feet high in places; shrubs, strung with autumn cob-webs, loomed out of it, hump-backed. There was a shed at the end of the garden, obscured by an overhanging shrub that had gone ape, and a gloomy path wound away toward it, trodden by the three of them through the long grass.

The first time Barbara had seen the garden she

had said, 'Oh, super! Barbecues,' but Lloyd could think only of Stanley, hacking his way through the jungle to find Dr Livingstone.

He had left his bicycle in the side entrance, at the foot of the cowboy's ladder. The ladder was trembling. Lloyd looked up. On the top rung was a cowboy boot, with a huge backside wobbling above it like a lead balloon about to make landfall. Lloyd zipped through the side gate, guiding the bicycle by the saddle. The cowboy's van stood parked on the far side of the street and Lloyd saw what Ingrid had meant when she had described it as unmarked. Clearly at least second-hand, its original owner's name had been shiftily painted over and the number plates were splashed with mud. It was exactly the kind of vehicle to make a passing policeman pause and consider.

He was half-way down Sackville Street when he realized that he had no idea where Victoria Park was. Salman had pointed vaguely to the north-west, so if he kept heading in that direction he ought to find the park by accident if not by design. If it were large enough to play cricket in, it ought to be difficult to miss.

He had slowed down to work this out and did not notice that he had halted in the middle of an intersection, until a car hooted at him. He drew hurriedly into the kerb and immediately locked pedals with someone coming the other way.

'Looking for an early grave?' said the owner of the other bike. He seemed familiar.

'Victoria Park,' Lloyd said.

'Turn right and keep straight on – or do you always pull to the left?'

'I was just working out where I am,' Lloyd said.

'But you only live down there,' said the cyclist, pointing back along Sackville Street.

'How do you know?'

'I've seen you, and I deliver your papers. Anyway, you're in my class.'

Lloyd looked again. 'Sorry, I didn't recognize you with that cap on. You were on the same table as The Man Most Likely.'

'*Who*?'

'Saddiq.'

'Oh, him. Likely? He's been there and back again.'

'You were at middle school with him,' Lloyd said, flatly.

'No, his cousin does a paper round as well. Same shop. What's your name? I only know you as 87 Sack.'

'What?'

'Off the corner of your papers. I'm Christopher.'

'Is that your Christian name?'

'James Christopher. I'm not a Christian, I'm a humanist.'

'What's that?'

'Opposite of a vegetarian. I only eat people.'

'Lloyd.'

'Is that *your* Christian name?'

'Lloyd Slater.' Without discussing it he found that they were pedalling slowly up Aston Road, side by side. He recalled that Salman had referred to his gaggle as the Aston Road Under Eleven Eleven, although there had not been quite eleven of them and they seemed mostly to be under seven.

'Is Victoria Park up here?' he said.

'Right at the end,' James said. 'What do you want to go there for, the paddling pool?'

'Cricket. I met –'

'Oh God, you aren't one of them, are you?' James moaned, faintly.

'One of what?'

'A flannelled fool.'

'Who are you calling a flannelled fool?' Lloyd aimed a sideways kick at the other bicycle. 'Dismount and be dismantled. Choose your own weapons.'

'Choose your own tombstone,' James said. 'Leave it till tomorrow, eh?' he added pacifically. 'It'd be a pity to die on the first day of term; sort of takes the edge off things. They'll mark you late for the rest of the year.'

'Wouldn't I just get crossed off the register?'

'But you would be late, wouldn't you? The late Lloyd Slater. I knew him, Horatio.'

'Who's Horatio?'

'That's what Hamlet said about the skull.'

'What skull?'

'I dunno,' James said. 'But whenever you see a picture of Hamlet he's always got a skull.'

'So've most of us.'

'No, airhead, he's *holding* it. Maybe he just liked carrying it about with him, like Long John Silver's parrot.'

'Oh yeah, and the skull sits on his shoulder and says "Pieces of Eight! Pieces of Eight!" '

'Perhaps he had two heads, like Zaphod Beeblebrox.'

'How come one died before the other?'

Lloyd perceived that a quarrel with James Christopher would be a non-starter and a great waste of time. He would be a lot more valuable as a friend than a sparring partner. 'Look, take that back about flannelled fools and I won't kill you after all.'

'It's only a poem,' James said. 'By Kipling.'

'The cake man?'

'I don't think so. Something about flannelled fools at the wicket and muddied oafs at the goals. My Dad quotes it every year when the football season opens.'

'Who are the muddied oafs, Chelsea supporters? Is your dad a teacher?' There was something suspiciously literary about James's conversation.

'My mum's a lecturer, at the Poly. I expect he got it from her.'

They had suddenly run out of road. When James had said that Victoria Park was at the end of Aston Road he had meant just that. The way was barred by a length of green railings and a gate. Beyond the railings lay trees and flower-beds and between the tree trunks Lloyd saw a stretch of sunlit grass where little brightly-dressed children ran about; Salman's Eleven.

'In for a spot of child-minding?' James said.

Lloyd noticed that among the babies were four or five people of Salman's own height, and larger, who were actually playing something that resembled cricket. The little ones were doing the fielding.

'I think he uses them as retrievers,' Lloyd said. 'You joining us?'

'Not into flannelling,' James said, cheerfully. 'Anyway, Iqbal speak with forked tongue.'

'He doesn't mean it,' Lloyd said, thinking of Salman's oblique apology in the Co-op.

'Oh, sure, but we aren't mates or anything.'

'You know him?'

'We were at the middle school. See you tomorrow.' James turned his bicycle and coasted away down Aston Road. Lloyd went on into the park, pondering on what James had meant when he said that Salman spoke with a forked tongue; that he was sharp – which he certainly was – or that he was two-faced. As he approached the cricketers he began to ask himself just what kind of a reception he would get, but Salman saw him coming and waved.

'Meet the team,' he said. 'Habib, Imran, Graham, Said, Angus . . . you've met the rest; don't worry about names. Everyone answers to *Oi!*'

Lloyd inspected the team. Imran was built like an American football tackle, one who was already dressed in his padding. The bat, seeming as insubstantial as a fly swatter, was tucked under his arm. Salman took it away from him and offered it to Lloyd.

'You sure?' Lloyd looked nervously at Imran, mountainous and batless, but he only smiled affably and shrugged, like a volcano about to erupt, a shrug to dislodge boulders and uproot small trees.

'He doesn't mind,' Salman said. 'I always have to let new friends bat first in case I've offended them. It's so easily done . . .' He blew casually upon his fingernails. 'You left-handed?'

'No.'

'Pity, we could do with the practice. There's a dearth of Southpaws round here.' Salman deployed his fielders. The big ones came in close, the infants, who seemed to know by instinct or telepathy what was required of them, spread into an orderly crescent on the outfield. 'I'll bowl,' Salman said. 'That'll make up for being nice to you.'

Imran and the team grinned silently. Salman bowled like a missile launcher, straight and deadly, heat-seeking. Lloyd, who could only block the bouncers he didn't duck, wondered where Salman's strength came from. He was so thin that two of him wouldn't have outweighed Imran. Even with his sleeves rolled up there was no evidence of muscles in his arms, only what looked like a complex arrangement of pulleys and wires under his skin, but the deadly balls kept coming until Lloyd felt relieved rather than disappointed when he heard the stumps go behind him and he could return the bat to Imran, who was still grinning. It occurred to him that he had not heard a word from Imran.

'You don't play American football, do you?' he asked, holding out the bat.

Imran shook his head. 'Too rough,' he said, as Salman streaked lethally past on the way to his more lethal run-up, 'but there's a club in the city. The Sabres.' Imran lumbered back to the crease and Lloyd took his place at mid-on. Salman was on his way back again with the dedicated simplicity of a charging rhinoceros. Late-flowering dandelions quivered upon their stalks. Imran took a mighty swipe, the ball soared above the trees, and the stampeding outfield converged beneath it. Lloyd awarded Imran's six a high reading on the Richter scale. American football would be hopscotch compared to this.

Lloyd always tried not to be in the kitchen when Barbara was doing the cooking, on the grounds that what the eye did not see the heart did not grieve over. Barbara belonged to the Primitive School of cookery, assaulting vegetables as though they had to be slaughtered before they were cooked, squaring up to meat like a squaddie at bayonet practice; then she lost her nerve and turned the gas too low. Food came to the table pale and tough; what the eye had not seen the stomach could guess at.

But he had to come through the kitchen after locking his bicycle in the shed at the end of the garden. Although it was not yet quite seven, bad light had stopped play even in the park. Here in the garden, under the drooping shrubs, the day had already seeped away; the high backs of the houses in Sackville Street obscured what little light remained in the western sky where the sun was declining behind a bank of clouds. Rustling through the long grass that brushed his shoulders, Lloyd could see Barbara at the kitchen window holding up a fish by its tail and gazing at it thoughtfully.

'Is it dead?' he asked as he passed and Barbara jumped.

There were two more rubbery blue fish laid out on the draining board. Barbara was gutting them with a Stanley knife that Lloyd had last seen upstairs on the landing windowsill, with chisels and putty.

'Hello, Brain Damage,' Barbara greeted him. 'How does Ingrid cook mackerel?'

'With dill.'

'We haven't got any. I'll use celery leaves instead,' Barbara said. 'That'll taste about the same, I should think. Where've you been?'

'Playing cricket.'

31

'In the street? How common. What will the neighbours think?' Barbara was trying to needle him. She did not care what the neighbours thought, although she gave them a lot of things to think about.

'In the park with my friend Salman.' He felt pleased to be able to say that, and it was true, he thought. Salman had referred to *him* as a new friend.

'Oh, wow, pals already.' Barbara raised the Stanley knife and unzipped the dangling mackerel with one slash. 'Take that, you treacherous swine!' The mackerel stared at her impassively. 'Where'd you meet him?'

'Salman? At school.'

'How was it? Does Ingrid cut the heads off? I can't remember.'

'Yes, but not with that. She's got a proper knife for fish, the one with the red handle. School's OK.'

'But you only made one friend?' Lloyd had been thinking that even one friend was pretty good going for the first day at a new school in a new town. Then he remembered James.

'No, I didn't *only* make one friend. There's another guy, James Christopher, and Kenneth Lin and –'

'Kenneth-Lynne? Like Mary-Beth, Billie-Jean?'

'Lin's his surname. He's Chinese.'

'Chinese do it the other way round. It ought to be Lin Kenneth.'

'He's English Chinese. Him and Salman are friends.'

'And where does Salman come from?' Another slash. 'Die, foul fish.'

'Bedford,' Lloyd said. 'Where's Ingrid?'

'Putting her feet up. She's bushed. You might

have washed up before you went gallivanting off with the lads.'

'You mean *I* should have washed up *your* coffee mugs?'

'Why not? I have to dust, don't I? One third of the dust in this house is your skin. What about the girls, then, Virus?'

'Girls?'

'I thought it was a mixed school.'

'It is.'

'So what about all these rampant girlies, then?'

'They don't ramp.' Lloyd thought of Farida and Farzana. 'Look, we're not going to have *just* fish, are we? What about spuds and salad and that?'

'Spuds – if you peel them. Don't look like that. Who's going to peel them when I go back to York? You'd better get in training.'

'We managed all right without you last year,' Lloyd growled. 'I thought *you* were supposed to be cooking tonight.'

'While you played cricket. Listen matey, a new age has dawned while you've been out hunting dinosaurs. The New Man *cooks*. He *hoovers*. He changes *nappies*.'

'But it's your turn to cook. I'll wash up.'

'It's better when you don't. You never rinse things.'

'At least I wash them. You're supposed to *clean* fish. We could all get mercury poisoning from those mackerel.'

'I thought I heard merry voices,' Ingrid said, coming into the kitchen. 'I love to see my chicks chatting happily together.'

'You are a sarcastic old bat, Mummydearest,' Barbara said. 'Lloyd was just offering to peel the potatoes and I was saying it's no job for a man.'

Lloyd went to the drawer for the paring knife.
'Blackmailer,' he hissed as he passed the sink.
  'Chauvinist piglet.'
  'Lazy cow.'
  'Sloth.'
  'What lovely smiling faces,' Ingrid said.

'Frizzo?'

'Lloyd?'

'How's your arm?'

'What d'you know about my arm?'

'It's joined on to your shoulder. Hey, d'you know where Felixstowe is?'

'Suffolk.'

'On the end of Felix' leg. Boom boom. Steve said you'd bust it.'

'That was years ago.'

'Steve told me last week.'

'Yeah, but I bust it during the holidays, just after you left. I had the plaster off yesterday. It was all blue and thin and yuck. We had to scrape the dirt off.'

'Off the plaster?'

'Off of my arm, and there was all crumbs down inside it. This boy next to me at the fracture clinic, he was having a plaster off his leg. He'd got a biro, fifty p. and a pie chart down his.'

'A pie chart?'

'One of his mates posted his homework down it for a joke. Matthew Bacon's got a dog.'

'What sort?'

'Bull terrier.'

'Not a pit bull?'

'Wouldn't put it past him. I can just see Bacon going in for dog fighting.'

'Yes, him versus the dog. *Is* it a pit bull?'

'No, one of those bald-looking white things that comes to a point. He brought it down the rec on Sunday.'

'You been to the assault course lately?'

'Not allowed. After I broke my arm my mum went down there and had a look. She went barmy, said I wasn't ever to go there ever again and got round all the other parents to ban it.'

Lloyd, picturing the assault course, could well imagine Mrs Ferris having a turn when she saw it. 'What'll you do?'

'Wait till they've forgotten all about it. They'll soon find something else to have a mass sweaty about. I never told her how I really did it, actually. She thinks I fell out of a tree.'

'What *did* you do, then?'

'You remember that death slide we made, with that mini carabina off David's key ring, well, the wire on the slide was all rusted up and when the carabina stuck, I kept going. I landed on my head and my wrist.'

'You could have broken your neck.'

'Yeah,' Frizzo said casually. 'That's why I didn't tell her. Did you see the Giants last week?'

'Barbara was watching some junk on ITV. She's going back to York, soon. Then I'll watch it regularly, sort of establish a claim by the time she comes back at Christmas and Ingrid'll say, "But Lloyd *always* watches American football." Possession is nine-tenths of the law of the jungle.'

'Is it?' Frizzo sounded doubtful. 'What jungle?'

'It's a quotation from Kipling,' Lloyd said loftily, having recently learned it from James Christopher.

'What, the cake man?'

'No, not the cake man, the poet.'

'Ho, poetry,' Frizzo said, with scorn, and Lloyd remembered that poetry was one of the things they never talked about down at the assault course.

CHAPTER THREE

'What's that?' Kenneth hissed, looking over Lloyd's shoulder, toward the end of the lesson. Lloyd had drawn a serpentine creature all down the margin of his history notes and along the bottom of the page. At one end was a pretty-pretty face with horns, at the other a scaly tail coiled into several knots. In between nine pairs of legs stuck out at angles.

'My sister.'

'She at this school?'

'No, York University. She went back today. There's been a massive signal failure on the East Coast Line and York Minster's been struck by lightning again.'

'When my sister sings,' Kenneth said, 'worms come out of their holes to die.'

On the timetable, the period was listed as SAS

37

which hinted at abseiling and bloody mayhem, but in fact stood for Social Awareness Studies, in which people voiced acceptable opinions about racism, sexism and unemployment, while making a start on their maths homework which had been set at the end of the previous period. Today's maths had been tessellation, which involved inter-locking rectangles and could be passed off as doodling if Mrs Baird should inquire about what was going on.

'Mind you,' Lloyd said, 'she's going to smell a rat when she notices that twenty-seven people are all doing the same doodle.'

'Tell her it's our collective unconscious,' said Vlad the Impaler, from across the table.

'What's that?'

'Roll up for a look at the walking encyclo-paedia, Ladies and Gentlemen,' Kenneth said.

'It was invented by Carl Jung,' Vlad said, help-fully.

'Yes, but what is it?'

'I dunno, quite.' Vlad was less a walking en-cyclopaedia than a quiz book from which someone had torn the pages where the answers were printed.

'Isn't it all of us knowing the same thing without being told?' Kenneth asked.

'I thought that was instinct,' Lloyd said, 'like homing pigeons.'

'Who was Jung?'

'A sort of early shrink, wasn't he?' Vlad said, vaguely.

'What – like Freud? Funny how people suddenly started being shrinks. I bet there weren't any psychologists when Napoleon was around.'

'You mean if there had been he wouldn't have

been Napoleon, he'd only have *thought* he was Napoleon.'

'Like PE teachers,' Lloyd said. 'People suddenly started being PE teachers. There weren't any Victorian PE teachers.'

'Simple,' Kenneth said, 'all PE teachers arrived at the same time, from the planet Krapton.'

'Yeah, a huge sort of litter – no, spores. They all started as spores. They floated down to earth and the ones that landed in favourable conditions –'

'What favourable conditions?'

'Changing rooms,' Vlad said. 'Those ones developed at once in the humid atmosphere –'

'That's it. They germinated on moist socks.'

'Anyway,' Kenneth said, 'they can all do impossible things. Moron can hang by his knees from his own collar-bones.'

'But one touch of Kraptonite makes them weak and evil.'

'Must be a heck of a lot of Kraptonite about, then,' Vlad said.

'Do stop talking for five minutes, Kyril, and let the others do some work,' Mrs Baird said, unfairly. At the table he was the only one who was facing her. Vlad glowered. He kept very quiet about his first name because people would insist that it was really Cyril, which he did not care for; but of course it was in the register, and Mrs Baird was too new to the job to know much about public relations. Vlad was short for Vladimov. He smiled at Mrs Baird and showed his eye-teeth.

Kenneth took unscrupulous advantage of Vlad's appointment as scapegoat and muttered to Lloyd, 'What are you doing tomorrow morning?'

'Cricket practice.'

'In autumn?'

'Indoor nets – with Salman.'

'Eeeeeugh! Another good man down the drain.'

'I thought he was your dear old friend.'

'Not when he's playing cricket,' Kenneth said firmly.

''ich is a'out 'inety 'er cent o' the ti'e,' Vlad said, trying to communicate without moving his lips.

'What are you doing tomorrow, then?' Lloyd said, as they collected their books and files together.

'Swimming,' Kenneth said. 'Me and my brother always go on Saturday mornings. You can get in at half price down the leisure centre if you get a community card.'

'How do you get a community card? It sounds like Monopoly,' Lloyd said.

'At the leisure centre. Take your birth certificate to prove you're under sixteen or over sixty-five. It costs a fiver and then you can get into all sorts of things cheap.'

'Badminton and that,' Vlad said happily.

'Well, I promised to go to the nets,' Lloyd said. 'What about Sunday?'

'Chinese school. What about Saturday afternoon? I could meet you after cricket.'

'OK,' Lloyd said. He looked at Vlad. 'Where do you go, Russian school?'

'We're Ukrainians,' Vlad said loftily, and Lloyd, who had imagined that this was the same thing, excused himself and slipped away to find Salman who was in a different group for SAS, along with Anwar, The Man Most Likely.

*

Opening the front door next morning to fetch in the milk, Lloyd was poked in the eye with a folded newspaper as he bent down toward the bottles.

'We can't go on meeting like this,' James said, although it was only the second time they had coincided on the doorstep. Lloyd was usually in the kitchen when the paper arrived. 'You doing anything this afternoon?'

'I might be going swimming,' Lloyd said.

'I was going for a bike ride with this guy down our road, but he can't make it. I thought you might like to come,' said James, not at all coy about letting Lloyd know that he was A N Other.

'How far do you think you'll get?' Lloyd said dubiously, looking over James's shoulder at James's bicycle. There was a basket on the handlebars.

'That? I only use it for the paper round. The real one's at home – fifteen gears – well, you saw it the other day.'

'Could we go tomorrow?'

'Morning or afternoon?'

'Morning. I'm playing cricket in the afternoon.' Salman went to the mosque on Sunday mornings.

'Right, I'll call round at ten. We can do time trials on the ring road, there's a cycle track. I can't make it earlier, the Sunday round takes hours with all those supplements. My spine's slipping over sideways.'

Lloyd took the milk and paper into the kitchen where Ingrid was washing paint brushes at the sink.

'You haven't been decorating during the night, have you?' Lloyd said.

'Barbara was doing the ceiling in the upstairs loo,' Ingrid said, 'only she got called away –'

'By a friend.'

'Two friends, how did you guess. These have been stuck in an empty jam jar since Thursday morning, and I mean *stuck*. If I can get them into working order we could make a start on the attic today.'

'Oh.' Lloyd had forgotten about the decorating. 'I was supposed to be meeting Salman for cricket practice this morning.'

'After lunch?'

'Well . . . Kenneth asked if I wanted to go swimming.'

'I see. I should have booked you well in advance. What about tomorrow?'

'James – he's the one who delivers our papers – he's just asked if I want to go cycling in the morning. It'll have to be in the morning because I'm going up the park with Salman again in the afternoon.'

'I thought you were short of friends,' Ingrid said.

'Only to start with,' Lloyd said, but that made him stop to think. In three weeks he *had* made friends; James, Salman, Kenneth; even Vlad the Impaler was friendly in spite of looking as if he might bite first and ask questions afterwards. On the other hand, there was something oddly formal about it all. They saw each other at school, no problem, but outside it was all appointments and arrangements. No wonder Ingrid talked about booking him in advance. He supposed he must be getting organized in his old age, though he rather regretted the free and easy days of the assault course with Steve and Frizzo and David, when no one ever organized anything. Perhaps he should dig out that diary Barbara had given him last Christmas, which had died of neglect on 11 January.

'Well?' Ingrid said.

'Eh?' He had forgotten that his mother was still standing by the sink, jam jar in one hand, brushes in the other.

'Are you going to be able to squeeze in a spot of decorating between now and Monday morning?'

'I don't have to be at the nets till ten,' Lloyd said. 'I could get started now.'

'That's uncommonly good of you,' Ingrid said. 'What about the shopping?'

'What about it?'

'We usually shop on Saturday morning. And don't you have any homework?'

'I did it last night.'

'All of it?'

'Most. Some. I'll finish it tomorrow, *really*.'

'OK, I believe you, but what about the shopping?'

'I can't do everything.'

'Neither,' said Ingrid, 'can I.'

'Anyway, why do we have to paint the attic today?'

'I was waiting for you to ask that.' Ingrid gave one last furious tug to the brushes. The handles jerked free leaving the bristles sprouting like grafted beards from the bottom of the jam jar. Ingrid hurled everything into the swing bin. 'That's something else to go on the list.'

'A new jam jar?'

Ingrid made throttling motions at his neck, hands dripping with white spirit. 'Does it count as infanticide after thirteen years? Look, pour the coffee and let's talk. You remember you said something about getting a lodger?'

43

'I was joking.' Of course he had been joking; and when he'd said that he would rather have a man than a woman he had been continuing the joke. What he would rather have was no one at all. 'Do we have to?'

'No, we don't have to. We could live on baked beans, if you like. I could sell the house and we'll go and squat in a Portacabin on the allotments. The rates came in yesterday. The point is, people are crying out for rented accommodation in this place, haven't you noticed the postcards in the newsagents? Now, we've got at least one spare room.'

'You're not going to put a postcard in the news-agents, are you?' He could imagine it. 'Young, male, smoker preferred?'

'I don't *prefer* smokers,' Ingrid said. 'In fact, I'd feel safer if he didn't. Less chance of setting the place on fire.'

'What about you setting the place on fire? It *will* be a him, then?'

'Well, actually . . .' Ingrid fiddled with a cigarette, 'there won't be any need for a postcard. You know I've done one or two jobs for the Poly?'

'Have you?'

'Yes, and I dare say there'll be more. Well, one of the art lecturers was talking to me in the canteen the other day – he's looking for a place. At the moment he's sharing with what he calls three psychopaths.'

'Really psychopaths? What is a psychopath, anyway?'

'According to the dictionary, someone with ab-normal social behaviour –'

'Ah! Barbara.'

'– due to chronic mental disorders.'

'A nutter.'

'That's one way of putting it. I think Paul's roomies are just chronically unpleasant.'

'Paul?'

'Paul Tyson. He's desperate to find somewhere else. It wouldn't be for long, he's buying a flat, but he got gazumped and now he's having to start all over again. I told him we might be able to help and I'd have a word with the interested parties. Barbara's all for it.'

'You asked her first?'

'I had to, before she went away. Then I had another think. It all depends on you, my son. Do the decent thing.'

'It's all right for Barbara, she won't be here. She'd probably rather have the psychopaths, anyway.'

'Say he stayed for three months, even. If it worked out we could get someone else afterwards. We'd have time to pick and choose.'

'You've decided, haven't you?' Lloyd said.

'More or less,' Ingrid admitted, 'but not if you really hate the idea.'

Lloyd suddenly did hate the idea. There were two students living in the house next door, but that had a basement and they came and went through a separate entrance under the front steps. This Paul Tyson would be part of the household, coming and going through their own door, up and down their staircase, sharing the bathroom; alien hairs in the soap. But he knew how much Ingrid was likely to get for letting the attic.

'Is he nice?' he said.

'Of course he's nice; no psychos here. He's so nice he's almost boring; quiet, respectable, engaged to be married – I mean, who gets engaged these days? – and wears a Greenpeace button. I think those are pretty good credentials, don't you?'

'When's he moving in?'

'Say ten days. You really don't mind, then?'

Doesn't make much difference whether I mind or not, Lloyd thought, but all he said was, 'We'd better make a start on the attic, then.' He was gratified to see how relieved his mother looked.

'In that case, nip up now with a bucket and wash the walls down. I'll be able to start after lunch, when I've bought some new brushes.'

'I'll help after swimming,' Lloyd said. 'I shan't be out *all* afternoon.' He knew this was the truth. When he and Kenneth had swum, the bathing party would go its separate ways.

The bathing party was more of a party than he had expected. As well as Kenneth and his brother there were a couple of cousins along, too, and an unknown neighbour who joined them un-expectedly at the deep end, rising unannounced from the bottom of the pool. When the session was over they all went off on bicycles talking to each other in what Kenneth had explained was Cantonese, although he spoke ordinary English to Lloyd and the cousins had Welsh accents.

Lloyd rode home alone.

When he got in, the house seemed deserted and chill, no sound of radio or typewriter. How nice it would be to have a dog that would run fawning and grinning to the door when it heard him coming, loving him best of all. He rinsed out his slip and the towel, hung them on the short line outside the kitchen door, and went up the two flights to the attic.

The second flight was steep and stark, without carpet or handrail. The door at the top stood open and as Lloyd came up the stairs he could see Ingrid, in the boiler suit that privately he thought far too trendy for someone's mother to be wearing, standing on a low stool to reach the attic ceiling.

'Getting the nasty bit done first,' Ingrid said. The ceiling area was very small, for the walls sloped toward it.

'Is he tall?'

'Who?'

'This Paul person.'

'I hope you're not going to call him that. About five foot ten, I suppose. I'm sure this room contravenes building regulations. We'll get someone shorter, next time.'

Next time. The rot had set in.

'Did you come back alone,' Ingrid said, 'or are there herds of friends downstairs?' She sat down on the stool and lit a cigarette. Lloyd frowned. 'My first since lunch.' Lloyd sniffed suspiciously, but all he could smell was paint. 'You know, you don't have to ask me before you bring anyone home with you,' Ingrid said. 'You never bothered before. *Chez* Slater's always been Liberty Hall.'

'It's different here,' Lloyd said. 'I was thinking that this morning. There used to be a whole gang of us; now everybody's separate.'

'That would be advancing age,' Ingrid said, 'or it could just be that the circumstances are different. Think about it; we lived in a small town – people here would probably call it a village. The fellows you went round with you'd known for years, since birth, almost. Play group, first school, middle school . . . if you'd gone on to the comprehensive it would have been the same old mob. I mean, there'd have been lots of strangers, but still about sixty of you from the same school.'

'It's like that here. A lot of people knew each other before, but they don't seem all that friendly – not with each other.'

'Maybe they've known each other long enough to realize that they don't actually like each other very much any more,' Ingrid said. 'It's a trying time, everyone's feeling stirred up. You'll sort yourselves out eventually.'

'You have to be forty-two to say things like that,' Lloyd said.

'When you're forty-two you'll see that I'm right.'

'Where are all your friends, then?'

'Back home – no, we mustn't say that. This is home. I'm in the same boat as you are, in case you hadn't noticed, starting all over again, getting to know new people – one at a time.'

'How does Barbara manage, then?'

Ingrid was still sitting down but Lloyd could see that she was thinking on her feet.

'Well ... how many of Barbara's friends are actually *friends*? They all use the same slang, dance in the same clubs, drink in the same pubs, wear the same clothes – and I mean the same clothes. I swear I never bought half the stuff Barb comes home in. But friends? They're just creatures of the same species who happen to be in a flock.'

'Hyenas?' Lloyd suggested.

'Don't be bitter.'

'Lloyd?'

'The same! Who's that?'

'Me, you drongo. David. I rang on Friday –'

'I was playing cricket.'

'And Saturday morning.'

'Still playing cricket.'

'And Sunday –'

'Sunday morning?'

'Don't tell me. Cricket.'

'Not in the morning. I was doing time trials on the ring road.'

'Timing cars?'

'No, I was with this mate James, from school. We took our bikes, there's a cycle track all the way round.'

'On a ring road?'

'It's because of the Polytechnic, it's on three sites. All the students use it and there's this really great stretch on the other side of town, dead straight and dead flat, like the Great Salt Lake.'

'Did you do it properly, with a stop-watch?'

'James has this stop-watch button on his digital, but then this bloke came by with a cycle computer.'

'How can you get a computer on to a bicycle?'

'You tow it behind on a low-loader. It's not *that* kind of computer, goon. It clips on to the frame. Well, he saw what we were doing and he stopped and offered to time us properly, so we took turns to race him. It was fantastic, this thing, there was a cadence monitor to measure pedalling speed, and a pulse sensor –'

'What, to make sure you're still alive?'

'It measures your heartbeat,' Lloyd said. 'He had it clipped on his ear lobe.'

'Wasn't giving him a brain scan, was it?'

'That was serious cycling,' Lloyd said. 'All that lot comes to over a hundred pounds. I looked it up.'

'My whole bike didn't cost a hundred pounds.'

'Nor did mine, but I'm going to get a new one soon. Twenty-three inch frame, next time. I think I've grown since I came here.'

'I've got a twenty-three already, it was second hand, though. You heard from Sutton, lately?'

'Why, what's he done?'

'He's going out with Frizzo's sister. You know, the one with the funny arms.'

'What d'you mean, going out?'

'Well, sitting in the bus shelter down by the King's Head. He's not much good at it, though. Every time someone comes past he shifts up and pretends he's waiting for a bus. Doesn't fool anybody,' David said. 'There aren't any buses after half past six.'

CHAPTER FOUR

Anwar, The Man Most Likely, had never before condescended to speak to Lloyd, but today their bicycles were anchored alongside each other. As Lloyd bent to open his lock he noticed that Anwar was busy with his own theft-proof device which was made of sterner stuff and looked as if it would take a thermal lance to break it open.

'Saw you last Saturday,' Anwar said. Lloyd felt obscurely flattered to be noticed by The Man Most Likely, as if a VIP had stepped aside from his red carpet to address a random member of the cheering crowds. It was only four o'clock and already he needed another shave.

'There's a lot of me about,' Lloyd said, as casually as he could. 'Where was I?'

'You mean you don't know where you were?' Anwar said. 'There's a word for that.'

'Amnesia,' Salman said. He was waiting with Vlad the Impaler for Lloyd to join them. 'You know how it is, "Sorry, officer, I don't know where I am. Everything went blank. When I woke up there was this gentleman beside me with his head wrapped round my axe." '

'And what exactly was Sir doing with an axe at three o'clock in the morning outside Sainsbury's?' said Vlad.

'I was waiting for them to open, officer,' Salman said. 'I wanted to buy some bread.'

'Fair enough, Sir, but that doesn't explain about the axe, really, does it, Sir?'

'I had to cut the bread, didn't I?' Salman said. 'Look, come on, Slater. I suppose that *is* your bike, isn't it?'

'D'you think I don't know my own bike?' Lloyd said, crossly. He had just looked up and noticed that Anwar had gone, without waiting for an answer; not surprising really, when he considered how Salman and Vlad had hijacked the conversation. The chance to strike up acquaintance with The Man Most Likely might never come again.

'I'm sure you know your own bike,' Salman said. 'I just thought you might be trying to nick someone else's.'

'That's not funny,' Lloyd said, more angrily than he had intended, for at that moment the recalcitrant lock sprang open and nipped his thumbnail; but it wasn't funny. Someone – or several ones in cahoots – made well-planned and successful raids on the bicycle blocks during lesson time. No one had yet lost a whole machine but so many parts had been liberated that, according to rumour, somewhere a new bicycle was being constructed out of spares, and almost anybody could be the culprit.

'I didn't mean it,' Salman said, perceiving that Lloyd was riled, and banging his head contritely on his own handlebars.

'Someone might hear you. Then what?'

'They wouldn't take any notice if they heard *him*,' Vlad said. 'They'd just think he was winding up. Didn't you notice in Latin this morning, when old Maitland said "Salvete, pueri et puellae", Salman goes "Salve tu quoque, Magister" and Maitland said "Would you mind repeating that?"'

'What's it mean, then?'

'Hello to you too, Sir,' Salman said. 'I suppose he wondered how I knew something he hadn't taught us. Typical teacher.'

'He assumed you were being rude,' Vlad remarked. 'I wonder what he *thought* you said.'

'I don't know enough Latin yet to be rude in it,' Salman said, regretfully, as they scooted down the drive. 'I worked it out from the word list at the back of the book. I thought he'd like that.'

'It's not what you say it's the way that you say it,' Vlad said. 'People like you can get sued for saying Good Morning. *Gor*, look at that! Who's he picked up this time?'

Ahead of them, as they came out of the gate, Anwar was pushing his bicycle beside a girl they had not seen before, a wonderfully willowy girl wearing red striped stockings.

'She's not one of ours, is she?' Lloyd said. 'I'd remember those legs if I'd seen them before.'

Vlad said, 'How does he *do* it? She must be eighteen.'

'She is. That's his sister.' Salman sounded scandalized. Lloyd looked sideways at him and saw that under his fringe of hair he was scowling with disapproval. 'They don't even go to mosque.'

'Don't they?' Lloyd tried to list the people he knew who went to church. No one, and neither did he, but though he could not share Salman's outrage, or understand it, he could understand the reason for it. It struck him now that this was the first time he had seen a Muslim girl wearing a skirt – it was quite a short skirt, and her hair was short too, bouncing on her shoulders as she strode beside Anwar's bicycle. He thought of Farida and Farzana, in his own class; of Mrs Hussain, next door but one at home, glimpsed occasionally through the leaves of trees in her garden, as she hung out sheets and baby clothes on the washing line. The first time he saw her, an insubstantial, brilliant fluttering beyond the dark branches, in her golden tunic and veil, he had surprised himself by noticing how beautiful she was. She was also very shy. He could not imagine her bounding along the streets like Anwar's sister, in scarlet stockings.

The two of them turned off down a side-street, long before the others had reached the corner of Stamford Road, and Salman recovered his good humour. 'See you at the nets, tomorrow?' he asked, as they parted. He and Vlad went to the left, Lloyd to the right.

As he wheeled his bicycle down the garden to the shed he noticed little Mrs Hussain in her garden, on tiptoe to reach the row of Mr Hussain's socks which hung at the very end of the line. She was wearing pink today, and the long plait of black hair gleamed between her shoulders. As she turned to drop the socks into the laundry basket their eyes met. Lloyd waved and called

'Hello?' Mrs Hussain lowered her eyes, modestly. He thought he saw her fingers flutter in return, but in the same movement she drew her veil over the shining hair and stooped to pick up the basket, leaving Lloyd slightly embarrassed but feeling old and worldly. In her eyes he was a man already, not a boy to be waved at.

At the same time he suspected that it might be impossible to be friends with both Salman *and* Anwar. Perhaps Anwar kept out of his way because he went round with Salman?

When he came through the kitchen he heard footsteps on the stairs, four feet ascending, out of synch and stomping, as though the owners were carrying something heavy. For some reason this made him think of undertakers and he visualized two men in black, manoeuvring a coffin round the bend in the stairs. He could see them so clearly, whiskery Victorian types wearing frock coats and crape-draped top hats, that it came as a shock when he looked up through the banisters to see two pairs of trainers and legs in jeans. He went on round the newel post for a proper look and discovered two young men stalled uncertainly where the stairs turned and carrying not a coffin but a draughtsman's table. The man nearer to Lloyd had an anglepoise lamp under his arm as well, and it looked as though everything, men and furniture, was on the verge of avalanching back downstairs. Lloyd swung round the newel post, sprinted up behind them and grabbed the lamp as it began to writhe intractably from under the arm that held it.

'Thank you, whoever you are,' said the owner of the arm, not daring to look round.

'I'm Lloyd.' He stepped back as the table recommenced its ascent. 'Are you Paul Tyson?'

'No, I am,' said the man at the other end of the table. 'That's Fred.' Some fancy footwork followed and the table reached the landing. Lloyd noticed a brown graze on Ingrid's new paintwork.

'How are you going to get that up to the attic?'

'Good question,' Fred said. 'I think we shall have to saw it in two.'

'Cool it, Tiger,' Paul said. 'No half measures with this guy. Saw it in two, chop it up, burn it down, that's his answer to everything. The man's a maniac. We'll unscrew the legs.'

'Do you want a screwdriver?' Lloyd said.

'Got one, thanks,' Paul said, and whipped it out of his back pocket. 'No, I don't go round habitually armed with a screwdriver, I brought it along specially. The legs are meant to come off, only Rockfist Rogan here *would* try and get it moved in one piece.'

Lloyd took a good look at Fred for the first time. Standing as he was at the head of the stairs he seemed enormous, looming like a statue viewed from the foot of its plinth, but he must be enormous anyway, six feet two at least, seventeen or eighteen stones; it was a wonder that he himself had not become jammed at the corner. Just now he was shifting from foot to foot, shamefaced, like a bad child caught out, and eyeing the mark on the paintwork. Lloyd ran his finger along it.

'We'll make good, don't worry,' Paul said. 'Anyway, it's me that's moving in, not him.' He turned the table on its side and knelt to attack the brackets underneath. '*I* don't plan to wreck the joint.'

'Where's Ingrid?' Lloyd said. 'We've still got

some of that paint – I could touch it up before she sees it – I mean, she only finished doing it the other day.'

'Give me the paint, I'll do it,' Paul said. 'I promised faithfully that she'd never know I was in the house. Fine start this is. I think she may be at the library. She dropped in at college this morning and gave me the key. Didn't she warn you there'd be strange men about?'

'I thought she said tomorrow.'

'I'm moving in tomorrow, but as I was free this afternoon I thought I'd shift the awkward stuff.'

'Actually, that was because *I'm* free this afternoon,' Fred said. 'He couldn't manage on his own. I don't know why I hang around with him, to tell you the truth. He just uses me as a block and tackle.'

'Can I carry anything?' Lloyd asked. It seemed that the sooner Fred left the premises, the better.

'That would be a help,' Paul said. 'We left the car outside – the boot's unlocked. Bring up anything that's in there – except the helmet. Thanks.'

'I'll take the lamp,' Fred said to Lloyd, who was still holding it, and lowered a massive arm over the landing banister. The anglepoise dangled helplessly in his grip and the shade drooped beseechingly on its jointed neck. 'Don't leave me with this dangerous oaf,' it seemed to plead, as it reached the bottom of its swing and cracked Lloyd across the bridge of his nose. He went downstairs faster than he had meant to.

The car was parked half on the pavement and blocked the front gate. Lloyd, coming in by the side entrance, had scarcely noticed it before. Most of the cars in the street were left like this because of the double yellow lines; few of the houses had garages. He climbed over the wall and opened the boot. Inside was a holdall with saucepan handles poking out, a box of tape cassettes, a wastepaper bin packed with crockery wrapped in newspaper, and a pile of sweaters fastened by a pair of bootlaces knotted together. Lloyd lifted out the saucepans and the sweaters. Underneath them was an orange dome, the helmet that Paul had asked him to leave there. At first he thought it was a crash helmet; on either side were painted tigers' heads with yellow eyes and yawning fangs; sabre-toothed tigers, and he recalled Salman's friend Imran telling him that the local American football team was called the Sabres. Of course; Fred. Never mind his being used as a block and tackle, he must block and tackle all the time. Given his size, he probably *was* a tackle. Lloyd put down the saucepans and reverently lifted out the helmet. He was right; attached to the front was the face guard; no crash helmet had that; he felt a brief pang of regret; if only it were Fred who was moving in.

'No – not the helmet. That's Fred's,' said Paul Tyson. Lloyd looked round and saw him climbing over the garden wall.

'You don't play as well, do you?' he asked hopefully.

'Come off it,' Paul said, 'look at me. I'd break in half. Is there a spanner in there by any chance? There's a nut on that thing as well as screws.'

'Is he a professional?'

'Ain't no such animal over here,' Paul said. He looked at Lloyd. 'Don't tell me you're one of them.'

'One of what?'

'An American football freak.'

'I watch all the games I can on telly. I want to play.'

'I thought I saw a cricket bat in the hall?'

'Yes, but I do other things too. Look – there's a spanner on the dashboard, under the gloves. Cricket and swimming and cycling. I'm going to start badminton next week, there's a club at school.'

'You get around, don't you?' Paul said. He opened the passenger door and stretched across for the spanner. 'What do you concentrate on?'

'I don't know, yet. See, we only moved here a little while ago. I was at middle school before, we never did things *seriously*, there were never enough people who could play anything really well.'

'So you never found out how good you might be? No worthy opponents?'

Lloyd had not thought of it like that. He and Paul shared out the luggage between them and closed the boot. 'We'll have to take it round the side,' Lloyd said, looking at the blocked gate. 'I can swim four hundred metres, and I dive . . . *safely*, not brilliant or anything. I wouldn't want to do it competitively. I just enjoy it. And cycling, that's just for pleasure, I mean, I do time trials with my friend and that, but I don't want to race. Salman says I've got talent at cricket. I think he knows what he's talking about.'

'Who's Salman?'

'My friend from school.'

'Is he the one you go swimming with?'

'No, that's Kenneth, and I cycle with James.'

'A different friend for every sport; you *have* got yourself well sorted out. Who do you play badminton with?'

'I haven't started yet,' Lloyd said, 'but when I do I'll probably play with Vlad the Impaler.'

'*Who?*'

'Kyril Vladimov. We call him—'

'Yes, yes. I can guess.'

'He plays all the time. I may not be good enough for him.'

'And who do you play football with?'

'No one, yet. Oh, do mind the paint,' Lloyd cried as they reached the stairs. 'I don't play at all, but Imran —'

'*Must* be a cricketer.'

'Yes, but he's nearly as big as Fred. He said there was a club in the city. Does Fred . . .?'

'Fred belongs, yes.'

'Fred belongs to what?' said Fred. He was sitting at the foot of the attic stairs, his knees drawn up, huge hands dangling between them, a walrus in pensive mood.

'The Sabres,' Paul said. 'Lloyd here was expressing an interest.'

Fred became animated at once. 'Do you play?'

'Calm down. Mind the paint,' Paul said. 'Mind the foundations. Remember, this is not your house.'

'I didn't do anything.'

'You stood up. See how the lamp is trembling.'

Lloyd glanced down at the anglepoise lamp which quivered upon its stem. It seemed to have a healthy fear of Fred.

'*Do* you play?'

'Not yet, but I want to.' Lloyd felt very foolish, someone of his size and height, standing before enormous Fred and talking of wanting to play American football.

'Why don't you join the club, then?'

'Join the Sabres?'

'There's a junior training session – mostly practice, no equipment involved, but it would be a start.'

'How do I join?'

'Just turn up. They play at the Riverside Sports Complex, six-thirty till nine-thirty, Wednesday evenings. It's a pound a session, you don't have to join until you've made up your mind about it.'

'I may not be any good.'

'Can you run?'

'Sprint.'

'Well, there's no long-distance involved, is there? You look in good shape.' Coming from someone of Fred's shape that might or might not have been a compliment. Lloyd wondered if, unknown to himself, he already showed signs of developing along the same lines.

'Do I just come along, then? I don't have to apply or anything?'

'Why don't you take him along yourself, the first time?' Paul said, kindly. 'You could pick him up here.'

'Good idea,' Fred said. 'That OK with you, Lloyd? You don't have to ask your mum or anything?'

'Oh no.' Lloyd was not entirely sure about that. Certainly he would not have to ask permission, but Ingrid was beginning to raise eyebrows at his multiplying sports fixtures. She showed an obsessive interest in his homework.

'I'll bring you home, too, if you like,' Fred offered. 'This time, at any rate. There's a bus stop just outside. You won't have any trouble getting there and back.'

Lloyd was considering how to convey his appreciation without sounding completely over the top, like Barbara, when a footstep and a closing door were heard below. All three of them jumped, guiltily.

'Ingrid?' Paul asked.

'The paint!' Fred said.

'Stand in front of it,' Lloyd said, and Fred surged down a step or two.

Ingrid's voice called, 'Paul? There's a traffic warden on the corner, proceeding in a westerly direction. You'd better move the car.'

Fred took off downstairs with unlikely grace for a man of his bulk, and they heard surprised squawks as he encountered Ingrid in the hall.

'She hasn't met him before,' Paul explained. He edged along the wall until he was standing in front of the skidmark on the paint.

'He's not at the Poly?'

'Works in the music shop in King Street, can't think of the name, you know the one, next to Marks and Sparks. Look, what shall I do about this?'

'There's paint on the window sill in the loo. Hang on, I'll fetch it.'

'No, I'll fetch it. You go down and make innocent conversation.'

Lloyd met Ingrid in the kitchen doorway. She still looked shaken.

'Who on earth was that?'

'Fred. He's helping Paul move in.'

'Oh good, is that all? I thought he might be planning to move in as well.'

'He plays American football,' Lloyd said.

'Yes, well, I don't quite see him on *Come Dancing*,' Ingrid said. 'I take it you've met Paul.'

'I've been helping him to move his stuff.'

'Like him?'

'Yes. Yes, he's nice.' But the best thing about Paul was Fred. No Paul, no Fred, no American football. Definitely Paul was a good thing.

'Rah! Rah! Rah! I'm joining an American football club.'

'You mean the Dolphins are signing you up?'

'Naff off, Sutton. There's a club here in the city, the Sabres. They have a sort of junior training session, and this guy who's moved in, well, his friend –'

'Hang on. What guy who's moved in? Living in your house, you mean?'

'Yes. He came this morning – well – last night –'

'Your mum's boyfriend?'

'No!' Lloyd laughed, but he was startled. The idea had never crossed his mind. 'He's our lodger.'

'Har har.'

'No, he is. He's renting the attic while he buys a flat. It'll only be for a few months, but we may get someone else after that. No, listen, his friend Fred actually plays for the Sabres, and he said he'd take me along.'

'What's he like?'

'Huge. Eighteen stone I should think. He's a tackle.'

'Not him, the other one. The lodger.'

'He's called Paul Tyson. He's all right too. Hey, you know you said you were getting a Wilson –'

'I already got it.'

'It's not your birthday yet . . . is it?'

'Last Tuesday.'

'I forgot.' Lloyd was horror-stricken. He had never before forgotten Stephen's birthday. They had been exchanging gifts for years, a kind of ritual. Whatever Stephen gave Lloyd in March, Lloyd gave Stephen in October. 'I owe you a cricket ball.'

'It doesn't matter.' Stephen sounded hurt.

'Of course it does. Look, I'm sorry. I just lost track of the date.'

'Doesn't *matter*. I expect I'll forget yours next year.'

'That'll even things up. Well, anyway, that Wilson, d'you know how much it cost?'

'Of course not, it was a present.'

'Yes, but you might have just noticed by accident. Didn't you go and look at it in the window, to make it feel wanted?'

'The one in the window's a practice ball. That was about a tenner. Anyway, won't they have a ball down there if it's a club?'

'It would be nice to have one to play with other times.'

'Oh yes. With all your new friends.'

'I don't know.' Lloyd was on the defensive, still feeling guilty about the forgotten birthday. It *did* matter, whatever Stephen said. 'I can't find anyone else who's interested. I mean, a lot of us watch on Channel 4, but I don't think anyone wants to play. I thought Imran might, you know, the guy I meet playing cricket –'

'You *still* playing cricket?'

'Indoor nets. Imran's built for American football. I think he'll look like Fred in a few years, but he didn't want to know. I was down at the nets this morning – hey, what's all this about Frizzo's sister?'

'What about her?' Stephen's voice became truculent.

'Someone said you'd been taking her out.'

'*Who* said?'

'Can't remember.'

'Wasn't David Hitchcock, was it?'

'Don't think so,' Lloyd said, mendaciously. 'Look, I'll ring you next week – on Wednesday, after football. Let you know how I get on . . .'

CHAPTER FIVE

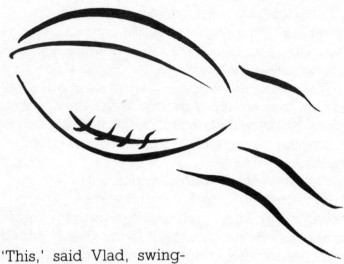

'This,' said Vlad, swing-
ing his racquet like a man
with murder on his mind,
'is Children's Hour. This
is not serious, man. It's Play School.'

He was referring to the inaugural session of the
badminton club, and Lloyd found it hard to dis-
agree. There was room for two courts in the
gymnasium, and more than thirty people had
turned up, hoping to play.

'I mean, what are they here for? I can count the
ones who can actually play on the joints of one
finger. Half the others don't even want to learn.
They're just mucking about.'

'Perhaps they just aren't very good,' Lloyd
said.

'At this rate they never will be. Look at those
Fifth Years, they're too old to be beginners,
they're just spoiling it for the rest of us.'

The Fifth Years looked as though they had come along with just that intention. The teacher in charge had twice told them to get off the court and make room for others, but somehow they always came back again, like malaria.

'Perhaps *I* shouldn't have come.'

'Oh, *you're* all right,' Vlad said.

'I haven't played before.'

'I think you'll be good. Tell you what, why don't you get one of those community cards and we can play at weekends – take turns to book the court? And after school, so long as we're finished by seven-thirty.'

Lloyd felt his self-esteem flex its biceps.

'You don't mind playing with me?'

'No. I said, I think you'll be good. At least you know which way you're facing,' he added, causing Lloyd to deflate slightly. 'How about tonight?'

'I can't, tonight. I'm going to American football.'

'Not you as well!'

'As well as who?' Lloyd said hopefully.

'Everyone's always on about it.'

'No one plays, though.'

'Not really surprising, is it? It's like chess played by all-in wrestlers.'

'I don't know. It could catch on. I think it just needs someone to get things started.'

'Ah, yes. The sheep principle,' Vlad said.

Ingrid was not particularly enthusiastic either about his plans for the evening, although this had nothing to do with sheep.

'Now, hang about,' Ingrid said, when Lloyd announced that he would be going out again at six o'clock. 'You amble in at ten to five because you've been playing badminton, and now you propose to take off for the rest of the evening. What about your homework?'

'I'll do that *now*,' Lloyd said. 'I've got over an hour before Fred comes. I did tell you about the football – no, I *asked*. I did. You said yes.'

'But what about dinner?'

'I'll get some fish and chips on the way back.'

'Suppose I've already prepared something?'

'You haven't . . . have you?'

'Suppose I *have*?'

'You haven't, though.' They stared each other out across Ingrid's typewriter, waiting to see who would crack first.

'What makes you think I haven't?'

'What are we having, then?'

Ingrid cracked, but only a little. 'All right, I know I said you could go, but I thought you'd be home earlier. Is this going to happen every Wednesday? Didn't you say lessons stopped early anyway, for sports clubs?'

'They did, but the badminton was such a shambles that Vlad and I and some others hung on till the mob had gone, they were just there to mess around, most of them, and then we played properly, but the caretaker says we can't do it again. I'll play out of school with Vlad, in future – and not on Wednesdays.'

'Is that Vlad as in Impaler?'

'That's what we call him,' Lloyd said. 'His name's Vladimov, but he could easily be a vampire. It's his teeth.'

'Goes down the outside of buildings head first, does he? OK, I'll give you the money and you can get us both some fish when you come home.'

'What about Paul?'

'What about him?'

'Shall I get him some fish and chips too?'

'I don't know if he'll be in,' Ingrid said. 'I've only seen him a couple of times since Saturday. I told him, if he wants to cook he can use the kitchen, but he has an evening meal at the college before he comes home. He made a very discreet job of that paintwork on the stairs,' she added, fixing Lloyd with a beady look.

'We hoped it wouldn't show.'

'It doesn't – now it's dry. I'm not quite a halfwit,' Ingrid said.

'It was Fred who scraped the paint.'

'Well, never mind. It's very nice of him to take you tonight – oh, by the way, I had a phone call from Jenny Sutton.'

'Stephen's mum?'

'That's right. What have you been telling him? She rang up quite out of the blue to ask how we were settling in.'

'I didn't know you were friends.'

'I met her once or twice. "I hear you've got a lodger," she said. "Nice to have a man about the house again . . ." Evil-minded old bat. I'd almost begun to forget what it was like to live in a place where everyone wants to know what everyone else is doing.'

'They might be like that here,' Lloyd said, 'only nobody knows us.'

'They're beginning to,' Ingrid said. 'Don't sound so pathetic; you'll make your mark.'

Lloyd was in his bedroom at the back of the house when he heard Fred's warning horn in the street outside. Racing along the landing he ran into Paul who came bounding down the stairs from the attic at the same moment. They bounced off each other. Paul was dressed for going out.

'Are you coming too?'

'To the gridiron? Not likely,' Paul said. Lloyd noticed that he was carrying a bouquet of roses, red and white. 'Fred's giving me a lift to the station, my battery's flat. I'm off to London, to see my lady.'

'Your lady?'

'My fiancée. Bianca.' They hurtled down the stairs, neck and neck. Lloyd picked up his sports bag, left packed by the newel post, as they swept past it.

'Does she live in London?'

'Dover. We meet halfway.'

Fred had both doors open by the time they reached the pavement, but he had parked in the road this time and a van, unable to pass, was quivering with impatience behind him. Fred, who had the engine running, lurched forward in a Le Mans start before they had the doors fully shut, as if they were making a getaway from a bank raid. Paul sat in the front seat. He flipped down the vanity mirror on the back of the sun vizor and began to rearrange his hair which had become dishevelled in the headlong descent, carefully sculpting it with a steel comb in the intermittent light from passing street lamps.

'Making yourself beautiful?' Fred inquired. When they halted at the traffic lights he looked back over his shoulder at Lloyd. 'You can see why he won't risk himself with any rough stuff, can't you. Who's a pretty boy, then?' he chortled derisively, as Paul nervously flicked his lapels in case of dandruff.

They let him out on the station approach.

Darkness was falling now, the booking-hall was brightly lit and Lloyd watched Paul force his way urgently through the mass of remorselessly advancing commuters who had just piled off a train from London. He held the sheaf of roses above his head like a bearer of the Olympic torch.

'Hope she's worth it,' Fred growled, as they drew away from the kerb.

'Haven't you met her?'

'Only met *him* a couple of weeks back,' Fred said. 'He runs my evening class; water-colour painting.'

Lloyd tried to imagine big Fred perched at an easel producing dainty pictures, but it was no harder than trying to equate Paul the lodger, college tutor who ran evening classes, with the romantic hothead who went galloping off to London – albeit on a Network Express – to meet his Lady Bianca.

He envisioned them flying into each other's arms at Paddington, he scattering roses, she with her long golden hair streaming behind her as she gathered speed.

Paul! Bianca!

Cathy! Heathcliff!

The Riverside Sports Complex was some way from the river, out on the industrial estate on the far side of the ring road. As they came downhill along the slip road, Lloyd saw the complex spread out below them; sheds, factories, car parks, under lurid orange sodium lamps. On the far perimeter a tall structure stood, surrounded by floodlit pitches, where running figures formed kaleidoscopes of multiple shadows which made them look like insects with many wings.

'Right,' said Fred, as they toured the car park, searching for a vacancy, 'when we get in you go and change. I'll show you where, and after that you just follow the crowd. There'll be forty or fifty of you. You start with a half-hour warm-up.'

'Are you playing tonight?'

'No, that was yesterday,' Fred said, to Lloyd's great disappointment. He had been hoping to see the real thing, although there was no telling how real it might have been. None of those floodlit pitches had been anything like large enough for a gridiron. 'I do weight training on Wednesdays,' Fred was saying. 'Can you see any gaps?'

'Over there,' Lloyd said, in time to prevent Fred from beginning a second circuit. 'Do you know if there'll be anyone from my school?'

'Don't know any of them,' Fred said, 'but I should think it's odds on you'll see someone you know.'

Fred was right. There were only two or three people left in the changing room when Lloyd arrived; total strangers; but when he got on to the field, which turned out to be a threadbare Rugby pitch with one and a half goalposts, he recognized one face immediately. It belonged to the Fourth-Year yoghurt eater who had tried to trip him up on the first day of term. It might be wise to give him a wide berth, in case he was a settler of old scores. Fred had said nothing about the likelihood of the evening ending with a scrimmage, but what an opportunity for a large, hostile opponent to settle an old score.

The session began with sit-ups and push-ups, a curious experience among fifty other people, rising from the miry grass and falling again like the briefly resurrected corpses of a slaughtered army; then practice sprints. Lloyd seemed to be dogged by the hefty presence of the yoghurt eater, but he showed no sign of wanting to renew hostilities. Either he had forgotten Lloyd entirely, or he had never noticed his face in the first place – or perhaps he was an oaf only at school; such behaviour had no place here, like spectator violence at a real NFL game. A fourth proposition occurred to Lloyd: was he himself known as a dangerous man, best avoided? He should be so lucky.

The warm-up ended with a jog round the field. After the first lap, Lloyd found himself in step with a boy of about his own age, who wore a sweatshirt with COLUMBUS printed across it, fore and aft.

'First time here?' Columbus asked.

'Yes; yours?'

'No, I joined last year – just before Christmas.'

'We only moved here in August.'

'You're not at my school, are you?'

'I dunno,' Lloyd said. 'Which school do you go to?'

'Highbridge.'

'North End.'

The conversation might have ended there by mutual consent, for Lloyd had already discovered that North End considered Highbridge to be a load of roaring snobs, mainly on account of their elaborate uniform and the catchment area; no one actually *knew* a Highbridge student personally. Possibly a Highbridgeite would not care to be seen in the company of a low-down North-Ender, but Columbus stayed alongside.

'That your name?' Lloyd asked.

'Columbus University. My brother got it in the

73

States, years ago. I've only just grown into it. Keith Mainwaring.'

'Lloyd Slater.' They shook hands, on the hoof.

'See you later, Slater,' Keith said, as a whistle sounded out on the field, and they all wheeled inward to where the coach was standing. This was the part Lloyd had been waiting for. So far he might just as well have been at school, in a PE lesson, except for the floodlights, but this was the beginning of the serious stuff. They were being sorted out into groups for practice at various positions. He had expected to be looked over and informed where he was to go as regarded size and weight, but it did not seem to matter, so he attached himself to the nearest crowd where he immediately located Keith.

'What are we doing?' he asked, as people showed signs of forming lines.

'Practice for wide receiver,' Keith said. 'You know what that is?'

'Yes, but I've never done it.'

'Those two guys in the middle are centre and quarterback. The other two are the wide receivers. We take turns at being cornerbacks see, in pairs, and we mark the wide receivers. When the ball's snapped – you know what that means –?'

'When the centre passes it to the quarterback.'

'Yes, well, the quarterback throws it to one of the wide receivers and the cornerbacks try to intercept – just the same as in a proper game, only there's no one else to get in the way. Then we all change round and two of us take turns at being cornerbacks while everybody else is a wide receiver. D'you get it?'

'Yes,' Lloyd said, doubtfully.

'Stick behind me and you'll see how it's done.'

Lloyd stood in the right hand line, behind Keith who was at the head, with a wide receiver beside him. Lloyd began to concentrate; this was the real thing at last. Just behind him, to his left, the centre snapped the ball to the quarterback; ahead of him the two wide receivers began to run, and suddenly Keith was no longer in front but running too, with his wide receiver, sticking close. The cornerback from the left hand line was the better marker and the ball went to the right. Keith strained to intercept it, but the wide receiver's hand sprang up and hooked it from the air as he made off at high speed toward the scuffed white line that marked the end zone. Keith and his opposite number trotted round to the back, the wide receiver returned the ball to the centre, and they were ready to start again. Lloyd found himself in front, the wide receiver at his side, and the ball coming in his direction. There was no time to consider tactics, he just kept moving and the ball sailed over, out of the wide receiver's reach.

'Now we change over,' Keith said, when the cornerbacks had each had two goes. 'We'll be wide receivers now.' Lloyd was about to follow him when he saw the coach waving in his direction.

'Not you – what's your name?'

'Slater. *Me*?'

'Yes, Slater, you. Carry on as cornerback for now.'

'Is that bad?' Lloyd muttered, as Keith moved away.

'No, you mutt, it's good. He must think you've got potential.'

Lloyd had not supposed that the coach had been paying enough attention to notice who had potential and who hadn't, but he was happy to go on being a cornerback. It was a pretty good start, all in all. He had imagined weeks of obscurity among strangers and yet here he was, on the first evening, already noticed by the coach and be-friended by an old stager; an old stager from Highbridge, at that. He decided that when he reported back, at school, on the glories of the evening, he would mention the Highbridge con-nection with caution, if at all. He might get duffed-up as a class traitor and a turncoat.

The evening ended with a game of sorts, rough and disorganized, exactly the kind of thing people imagined American football to be who did not know the rules. Lloyd was still keeping an eye open for the yoghurt eater, for if he still had a shot in his locker, now would be the time to fire it but, Lloyd noted, he prudently kept clear of any hard stuff. His metier was evidently hand-to-foot combat in school corridors; here he was just another player – not a very good one.

'How are you getting home?' Keith asked, in the changing room.

'My friend's giving me a lift. He's in the Sabres,' Lloyd said, pridefully. Surely Fred counted as a friend – he had acted friendly, hadn't he? It was too complicated to explain that actually he was the lodger's friend. Did Highbridgeites have such things as lodgers?

'I was going to say we could probably give you one,' Keith said. 'My father picks me up. Where do you live?'

'Sackville Street.'

'Oh, that end.' Lloyd wondered if he were

imagining the true ring of Highbridge scorn, but Keith went on, 'We go round by the ring road. We could easily drop you off.'

'Well, I'd better go with Fred this time, because he arranged it all, but after this I'll be coming by myself.'

'Fred? Not Fred Coles?'

'Do you know him?'

'Not personally, but – he's brilliant.'

Lloyd took it that Keith meant Fred was brilliant at football. Brilliance was not something he had thought of associating with Fred.

'I haven't seen him play,' he said casually.

'I thought you said he was your friend.'

'Yes, but I haven't known him long. I haven't known *anyone* long,' Lloyd said.

'We'll give you a lift back next week,' Keith said. 'Can you get down here by yourself? My father doesn't bring me, just takes me back.'

'I'll get the bus in,' Lloyd said, gratefully. He had been planning to nag Ingrid into letting him cycle down, but he did not think he would succeed, and he had not looked forward to hanging around the bus stop in the murky darkness on cold winter evenings.

'OK, see you next week.' They parted at the main entrance, and Keith was borne away in a car that stood waiting for him with its engine running. Lloyd sat down on the steps to wait for Fred. The car park was half empty now, a thin October mist had come up off the river and drifted across the industrial estate, gathering smoke and fumes as it passed, furring up the sodium lamps. Behind him he could hear echoes of footsteps, balls thudding on the indoor courts, voices calling, water splashing and gurgling in the showers; the best evening yet, since he came here. The coach had singled him out and so had Keith. No doubt Keith thought the more highly of him for knowing Fred Coles, but he had not been aware of that when he first approached Lloyd. He had just been friendly.

Better still, he had been on his own and had gone off with his father; he hadn't been surrounded by a pack of old mates he'd known since play school or been met by half-a-dozen brothers and sisters and cousins. He was on his own and Lloyd was on his own. Like had called to like.

'Is that Frizzo?'

'How did you guess?'

'I didn't guess, I worked it out logically. I dial Frizzo's number, someone who sounds like King Kong on helium answers the phone. Conclusion: I must be talking to Frizzo.'

'What are you on about?'

'It's a syllogism. We did it in English.'

'We're reading *The Thirty-Nine Steps* in English. *Again.*'

'I've been to American football practice – on Wednesday. Coach said I showed great promise. I played cornerback, all evening.'

'Sutton got a Wilson for his birthday.'

'I know. Hey, is he really going out with your sister?'

'Nah, they had a row. She said he ought to get his hair cut properly, 'cause it kept getting in her eyes –'

'In *her* eyes?'

'He must have come in close. So he said, why didn't she do something about her zits, so she hit him.'

'Where?'

'In the bus shelter. Half the school was watching.'

'This guy I go to American football with –'

'The lodger?'

'What do you know about the lodger?'

'Sutton's mum told my mum that your mum –'

'Well, it isn't the lodger. It's his friend, Fred Coles.'

'Who's he?'

'He plays for the Sabres.'

'Who're they?'

'Our American football team. He's almost famous – well, locally.'

'What's the lodger like?'

'He's called – oh! I just heard my mother come in. I'll ring you back, sometime. OK?'

'OK, see you.'

'You won't,' Lloyd muttered, hanging up. He had not heard Ingrid come in. She was in already, had been for hours, but there did not seem to be much future in that conversation. He dialled again.

'David?'

'Who's that?'

'Lloyd. I don't sound that different, do I?'

'You sound drunk.'

'Oh sure, I've been on the booze all day. We took a six-pack into RE.'

'You never.'

'Of course we never. I've been to that American football practice.'

'To watch?'

'No, to play. I told you – didn't I?'

'You didn't tell *me*,' David said. 'Last time you rang you were on about bicycles. I went down to Broadbent's on Saturday and looked at the cycle computers. You were right about the price.'

'The football was brilliant,' Lloyd persisted, 'well, no, actually it wasn't all that brilliant. I mean, there was about fifty of us. It was a bit chaotic really, but the coach –'

'That your mum's boyfriend?'

'*What?*'

'Sutton said your mum had a new boyfriend who played American football and he's living in your house.'

'Look, Ingrid rented our attic to a bloke from the Poly. He's engaged. He's *not* her boyfriend. Anyway, it's his friend who plays, not him.'

'All right. Keep your hair on.'

'And you can tell Sutton to keep his big mouth shut. Hasn't he got anything else to talk about?'

'Look, you needn't bother to ring if you're just going to shout at me.'

'Sorry,' Lloyd said. 'I'll have to hang up anyway. I just heard my mum come in.'

CHAPTER SIX

In SAS the sexism debate
smouldered from lesson to
lesson, occasionally burst-
ing into flames. Every time
someone tried to damp it down, so that they
could all get on with their maths, it flared up
again. Zoe De La Hoyde stoked it zealously. She
had indeed turned out to be The Woman Most
Likely to Make Waves, but not the kind of waves
they had all been hoping for. When the rest of
the group sullenly declined to furnish examples
of sexism, Zoe advertised her own experiences,
which were many. Sexism, as Vlad murmured
one morning, seemed to settle on Zoe like dust
on a television screen.

'For instance,' Zoe was saying, 'my brothers
help with the washing up and that, but they never
offer to, and my father, he's the same. They never
make a fuss about it but they always have to be

asked, like they were doing a special favour.'

'Which you don't, of course,' James muttered softly.

'What was that, James?' Mrs Baird asked, hoping that it was an intelligent contribution to the debate. James, who had been prepared for nothing of the kind, flapped his hands expressively. 'Thinking aloud,' he said. Mrs Baird had to be content with the notion that he was even thinking. Vlad, sitting next to him, came to the rescue.

'Well, all right,' he said, 'Zoe's dad's past help – no, hold on, Zoe; you said it, not me – but it's different for your brothers. It's got nothing to do with being male, really, has it? It's not sexism at all, in their case, it's childism. When you're a child you expect your mum to do things for you because that's what happens when you're a child. You don't suddenly turn into an adult and do it all yourself, do you?'

'I've always helped around the house,' Zoe began.

'Why?'

'My mother always –'

Vlad pounced. '*There* you are. You blame your dad and your brothers but it was your mum who brought you up to think that *you* were the one who has to do the washing up.'

'You leave my mother out of this,' Zoe snapped.

'You brought her into it,' Vlad said.

'All right; what about your mother then?'

'I do not expose my mother to vulgar public brawls,' Vlad said, superbly.

Lloyd had seen Vlad with his mother in town, and thought that Mrs Vladimov looked well able to handle a vulgar public brawl. He recalled, moreover, that it had been Vlad who was carrying the shopping.

The brawl was cut short by Mrs Baird, gratefully catching sight of the time.

'Right,' she said, with an inspirational smile, 'I think we've established the fact that prejudice is as much the result of unchallenged attitudes as active discrimination –'

'What *is* she on about?' Vlad demanded. 'It's the other way round.'

'Don't *say* anything,' James pleaded, 'she's only trying to get us out of here on time. You're the only one who's listening. Don't start another argument.'

'Has anyone got anything more to add? Any conclusions?'

'Rehouse the dead, I say!' Vlad called out. 'Society is to blame.'

'What I want you to do over half term is to begin thinking about racism in the same way . . .'

'Do you think she's got a list of isms?' Kenneth said. 'Working her way through them? Where'll we have got to by the end of term?'

'At the rate we're going we'll still be on racism,' Lloyd said. 'Are you swimming tomorrow?'

'I thought you'd be at cricket practice.'

'Only in the morning. I've got one of those community cards now. I can get in free before five o'clock.'

'We've got all week,' Vlad said. 'Let's play badminton on Monday. I'd forgotten it was half term. Terrible how time catches up with you. Do you remember how long the week used to seem when you were little, counting the days till Friday, even on Thursday. Years went on for ever. Teen-agers were old men.'

'Childism,' Lloyd said.

'Ageism,' Kenneth said. 'I wonder if she's thought of that one.'

'I suppose you're fully booked for Sunday,' James said when they were cycling slowly home down Aston Road.

'Not this week,' Lloyd said. 'I thought I might be staying with an old friend this week, you know, over half term, but nothing came of it,' he added. Stephen seemed to have suspended com-munications. In any case, if he went back, what would he be going back to? The allure of the assault course had faded. What would they all talk about if they met up again? Lodgers? What would they all *do*?

'I fancied a really long cycle ride, if the weather holds,' James said. October looked set to end in bright mornings with sharp thin frosts that whitened as the sun rose, giving way to mild yellow afternoons.

'Clocks go back on Sunday,' Lloyd said. 'Let's go out early and not come back till lunch.'

'Twenty miles each way?'

'Not really *long*, is it?'

'No, but the hills are,' James said, evilly. 'The hills make you want to lie down and die.'

'Why don't we go a different route, then?'

'I like hills,' James said. 'It's so nice when you stop. No, it *is* a good ride, lots of long straight stretches. There's only two really steep hills – we can test our gears. I'll do my paper round a bit earlier and call for you. Half past eight?'

James rode on and Lloyd turned along Sackville Street. James was some distance away when he looked back and yelled, 'See you Sunday, then. Up the Ists!'

'You what?'

'If the lesson's Isms, we must be Ists. Sort of secret society devoted to spreading social unrest.'

In the kitchen he tripped over a khaki holdall that someone had left lying in the doorway. He thought it was Paul's, although Paul was not normally one to leave his things lying around, but as he went upstairs, carrying coffee for himself and Ingrid, he heard voices coming down from the attic where Paul must have left the door ajar. One voice was female; could it be his golden Lady Bianca? He found it hard to think of quiet, plain Paul with anyone so gloriously exotic. He looked as if he ought to be married to a woman called Doris and drive a Skoda, but the car that he parked farther down the road was a dashingly ancient green Sunbeam Alpine, and upstairs was Lady Bianca. Lloyd paused on the bend in the stairs and frowned, remembering his vision of the undertakers; his imagination was getting out of hand again. The voice coming down the attic stairs was Barbara's, no lady she. He stormed along the landing and shoved open the door of Ingrid's office.

His mother, with her customary small blue cloud overhead, was scrabbling about in the filing cabinet, and turned when she heard the door creak.

'Barbara's just blown in for the weekend,' she said, before Lloyd could open his mouth. 'She turned up about an hour ago and said she couldn't last another minute without seeing us again.'

'She wants to get her washing done,' Lloyd translated. 'What's she doing upstairs?'

'She hasn't started on Paul already? I thought she was making her bed.'

'Come to think of it,' Lloyd said, perching on the desk to drink his coffee, 'she probably came home specially to give him the once-over. She'll eat him alive.'

'How elderly you sound. She won't make much impression on Paul, he faces a studio full of Barbaras every day. Are you going to do your homework now? I suppose you'll be busy tomorrow.'

'Cricket in the morning, swimming in the afternoon. I haven't got *much* homework, and there's a whole week to do it in.'

'A week? Oh God, half term already. I'd forgotten that. Well, keep Sunday free, will you?'

'What's happening on Sunday?'

'Paul wants to take us all out to lunch – as a token of his gratitude.'

'Gratitude for what?'

'The room, of course,' Ingrid said. 'He really was in a hurry to get out of that other place. His fiancée's coming over tomorrow evening, so we'll be quite a party. Mind you, he issued the invitation *before* Barbara showed up, but I imagine she'll have other friends to fry.'

'Is she staying here?'

'Who, Bianca? No, they've given her a room at the Poly – she's a guest lecturer; it's not just a social visit. Well, to be honest, I think the lecture is just an excuse – she's Paul's guest.'

'What does she lecture about?'

'Art, I suppose. Paul says she's a painter, but I imagine she teaches as well. It's a good thing I didn't offer her Barbara's room.'

'Won't she want to be with Paul?'

'I dare say, but the bed up there's much too narrow. Now, remember, don't make any arrangements for Sunday. Paul's booked a table for one o'clock.'

'I've just remembered something else,' Lloyd said, uncomfortably. 'I'm going for a cycle ride with James on Sunday morning.'

'Fair enough, but be back by eleven-thirty – no, say eleven. That'll give you time to have a bath and get changed and allow for you being half an hour late.'

'James thought we could go for a really long ride. I'd be back by one.'

'And leap straight from your steaming saddle into the foyer of the Royal Court Hotel? Oh no, you don't. The Royal may not be five-star cuisine but it's not a fast food joint either.'

'But I promised James –'

'Promised? A solemn oath? On your mother's grave? Listen Lloyd, I don't intrude much upon your social life, and I'm not going to offend Paul, so you can do *me* a favour for once. He needn't have invited you at all, but he likes you.'

'Barbara could go instead.'

'I'm not arguing.'

'Yes you are.'

'OK, I'm arguing. At this point I stop arguing. Just give James a ring and tell him you can't make it. As you said, you've got all next week.'

'He's going away for half term.'

'I am not arguing,' Ingrid said, and began to type, hard and fast. Lloyd turned away. He always felt particularly excluded when Ingrid was working in Finnish or Hungarian because it meant that she was *thinking* in a foreign language –

profoundly obscure foreign languages that could not even be guessed at, unlike Latin or French. It was the same when Imran and Salman spoke to each other in Urdu. They did it without thinking, not to shut him out, but he felt shut out all the same.

He went downstairs to the telephone in the hall, hearing Barbara's loony giggles upstairs in the attic. James's mother answered when he rang. 'I'll see if I can reach him,' she said doubtfully. 'I think he's out in the street.' There was a long silence, broken intermittently by tinny jingles from a television. Someone was watching a quiz show. Lloyd had not seen James's house but it sounded as if it must be a long way to the front gate. At last he heard footsteps.

'Yeah?'

'It's Lloyd. Sorry, were you busy?'

'Time trials – down to the end of the road and back.'

'Oh. Look, I can't make it on Sunday. We're going out. I didn't know until I got home.'

'That's OK.' James seemed surprised that Lloyd should have bothered to tell him. 'There's a whole lot of us going, my cousin and that. We shan't miss you,' he added, consolingly.

'Yes, OK. Sorry then. See you.' Lloyd hung up. Of course they would not miss him. The world was full of cousins. Kenneth had cousins. Most of Salman's cricket team were related to each other if not to Salman. Probably Vlad too belonged to a sinister network of Ukrainians. That just left Keith. Roll on Wednesday.

Lloyd thought that Salman looked faintly surprised to see him at the indoor nets next morning.

'Thought you'd thrown us over,' Salman said. 'Gone on to better things.'

'What things?'

'Oh, the Twin Set, the Blitz and the Dog. Be honest, Slater, you're just in it for the cheer-leaders.'

'Come off it,' Lloyd said, 'I've only been once. And it's only once a week, anyway. I'm not giving up anything else because of it.'

'You'll have to give up something next year,' Salman said, doomfully, 'when we start on the GCSE course work. Three hours homework a night, they said.'

'Will you give up cricket?'

'Not likely.'

'How will you fit everything in? Mosque school and Arabic and learning the Koran by heart –'

'I ought to have done that by this time next year.'

'Then what?'

'Then I've sent seven generations of my family straight to heaven,' Salman said.

Lloyd looked up sharply, thinking that Salman simply could not be serious, but it was Salman's turn to bowl, and he moved straight from his amazing statement into delivering a deadly leg-spinner that could take years off a batsman's life.

When he came home from swimming, Barbara was in the garden harvesting what looked like a year's supply of knickers and tights from the washing line. Apart from a high-speed exchange of insults on the stairs last night he had scarcely seen her since she had come home. From visiting Paul, who still looked slightly flattened by the impact, she had gone on to a rendezvous with friends, returning long after Lloyd had gone to bed. He heard her thundering upstairs again just as he was falling asleep. When he left home, this morning, he had aimed a retaliatory kick at her door as he went past.

'Hello, Health Hazard.' Barbara peered over the washing line at him with the wide-eyed look of a night bird. Given the chance she would have slept all day and risen at sunset.

'Hi, Sis.'

'How's it going, Bro?'

'How's what going?'

'Life, the Universe, everything. Ingrid says you're always out; you must be doing something.'

'I'm doing a lot,' Lloyd said. 'I've just come back from swimming, I was at cricket this morning.'

'When do you play American football?'

'Wednesday nights, but I'm trying to get people at school interested, so we can practise during the week.'

'Yes . . . all these squillions of friends. Paul says you've got a different friend for every sport.'

'You haven't been talking to him about me, have you?' Lloyd felt that his privacy had been violated.

'I only asked him how you were getting on.' Barbara jerked the washing line on its pulley. The peg bag shot up into the air and crashed to the ground.

'Why didn't you ask *me*? I know how I'm getting on better than he does.'

'I needed something to talk about,' Barbara admitted cheerfully, 'so I went and played at being the concerned big sister. I couldn't barge into his room and yell, "Hello, stranger, tell me all about yourself," could I?'

'You didn't have to barge into his room at all,' Lloyd said. 'Anyway, I'd have thought that's exactly what you'd do.'

'Too unsubtle,' Barbara said, as they went indoors. The kitchen sink was full of coffee mugs again. 'The best way to get people to talk is to ask them about someone else. Sooner or later they get round to talking about themselves; everybody does.'

'Is that what you've been doing all afternoon?' Lloyd asked, eyeing the sink.

'I just rang up a few fans and said, "Hi, folks, Barbara's back in town," and they all came running. Don't your friends come here? Paul said –'

'I wish you *wouldn't* ask Paul.'

'I don't suppose I'll get the chance to talk to him again, anyway,' Barbara said. 'His lady's coming over this evening. He's gone down to meet her off the train.'

'You going out to lunch with us, tomorrow?'

'No, I've arranged to meet some people,' Barbara said vaguely. 'But *don't* you have friends round? Ingrid said she never meets any of your mates.'

'I don't see why she'd want to. They wouldn't have a lot to say to each other, would they? She never has people round here. You really have been on a fact-finding mission, haven't you? I wish you'd mind your own business.'

'Don't lose your rag, Bro,' Barbara soothed him, in a voice precisely calibrated to stir him up. 'I just think she'd like it if you were home a bit more often.'

'That's good, coming from you,' Lloyd said. 'You're never here at all.'

'I can't be here, can I? I'll move out altogether soon, won't I? You *do* live here, you're part of the household. Do you think Ingrid likes being at home on her own?'

'She doesn't have to stay at home.'

'You'd love it if she went out all the time, wouldn't you?'

'I wouldn't mind,' Lloyd said, knowing perfectly well that he would. '*You're* going out tomorrow.'

'Yes, but I've been in all day. I did the washing –'

'*Your* washing.'

'And the sheets. I did them first, *and* ironed them. And hoovered right through. What did you do – apart from playing cricket and having lunch at the Wimpy and going swimming? You didn't even wash up this morning.'

'I would have,' Lloyd said, 'if I'd been asked.' He stopped. He had heard it all before.

'I'll wash up the coffee mugs,' he said.

'That's big of you,' Barbara said, ungratefully. 'You'd better put your bike away first. It's starting to rain.'

While they were arguing, the garden had grown dark. This time tomorrow, after the clocks had gone back, it would be night, autumn giving way to winter. The long grass was dying down and the path to the shed had become bald and muddy. Lloyd steered his bicycle in beside the wheelbarrow and fastened the door on it, gazing back toward the house with its warm windows. The light went on in Barbara's room and illuminated the ghostly flapping of Baby Hussain's napkins behind the bare branches on his right. Barbara came up to the pane and drew the curtains, closing him out. Simultaneously, the light went off on the landing. He made his way back to the constant glow of the kitchen window and found Ingrid burrowing in the cupboard under the sink.

'What are you looking for?' Lloyd asked, as Ingrid's arm reached out behind her to dump a pile of dusters and floor cloths at his feet.

'Spare light bulb. The one on the landing blew so I switched it for the one in the hall and now that's gone as well, and Paul's just come in with Bianca. She'll think I run a cheap lodging house. There's something about dud bulbs . . .'

'It's in the drawer.' Lloyd fetched it out, feeling enormously helpful and efficient. Barbara would not have known where to look.

'Can you reach to put it in?' Ingrid began stuffing all the dusters back again among the detergents and shoe brushes. 'Give it to Paul and he can fix it on the way up.'

Lloyd went into the dark hall, hoping for a glimpse of Lady Bianca, but she and Paul were already on the landing, out of sight. He called up through the banisters, 'Hang on, I've got another bulb here.'

'I'll come down for it.' The voice was soft and American. Lloyd seemed destined to confront reality on the stairs. He had not expected Bianca to be American. Then her arm came through the banisters to take the bulb, and it was black. Still thinking of golden hair, he was so taken aback that he forgot to give her the bulb, took the hand and shook it.

'How do you do,' he said, foolishly.

Beyond the banister Bianca laughed, and when Lloyd still hung on, her other hand came through and took the bulb. 'Here you are.' She must have passed it straight to Paul. 'I'm coming down to say hello properly, where I can see you.'

Lloyd stepped back into the kitchen as Bianca came round the newel post and down the hall. She really was black, with the darkest skin he had ever seen, but he had almost been right about the golden hair. She wore it in dozens of tight skinny braids, and every other braid was dyed blond. The effect was stunning. Bianca shook hands with Ingrid and smiled at Lloyd. He realized that he was still staring.

'My mother didn't know any Italian,' she said. 'She just thought Bianca was a pretty name.'

'It is. It suits you,' Lloyd stammered, and was almost overcome by a sense of his own gallantry. He felt like bowing.

Oh, Pretty Woman!

'Listen, Sutton, before you ask about the lodger –'

'I wasn't going to ask about the lodger.'

'His fiancée's here. We're all going out to lunch today.'

'Wow! Thrills! Is that what you rang up to tell me?'

'No, just to say hello.'

'Hello, old fruit.'

'I was going to ring up earlier in the week and tell you about the American football, but you were out both times I rang.'

'Dave Hitchcock says you rang him up on Thursday in a filthy temper.'

'I wasn't in a filthy temper when I rang him up, but he kept going on about the lodger. What've you been telling people?'

'What *was* the football like – look, I've only got a couple of minutes. Someone's coming round.'

'Who?'

'Just a friend.'

Lloyd detected a reluctance to elaborate. Had Stephen already replaced Frizzo's sister with someone more amenable?

'It's not very well organized.'

'What isn't?'

'The football practice. I mean, I enjoyed it, but –'

'I think that was the doorbell.'

'Can't your mum answer it?'

'She's not in. I must go. I'll call you next week. See you.'

'See you.' Lloyd tried to hang up first to show that he too had no time to waste in idle chat, but Stephen beat him to it.

CHAPTER SEVEN

If Sunday's telephone call had not been cut short Lloyd might have reminded Stephen that they had once planned to spend half term together. As it was, the days ahead confronted him like a row of empty boxes, each to be fitted and filled. It seemed that he had said farewell to the old days and the old ways. Barbara vanished again at first light on Monday morning, leaving her bedding strewn round the room. Lloyd virtuously stripped mattress, duvet and pillows, hoping that Ingrid would notice that he was being helpful, but Ingrid thought Barbara had done it and grumbled because she had not put them straight into the washing machine. Lloyd did not enlighten her.

Bianca was returning to Dover on Wednesday and Ingrid invited her to dinner on Tuesday night. They did it in style, linen tablecloth, napkins and candles. Lloyd sat opposite Bianca and all through the meal watched her shining smile behind the candles, the golden glints in her hair. On top of all that, she let slip during the evening that her brother Alphonse, back in Ohio, played college football, one of those solitary specialists, a kicker. Lloyd hoped to draw her out about Alphonse, but the conversation had been on less physical things; painting and Hungarian poetry, acid rain, elections, mortgages, so he had retired from taking part and in the end just sat looking at Bianca in the candlelight and wondering what she saw in Paul – apart from the fact that Paul was obviously a very nice man. Perhaps that was all it took.

On Tuesday he had played badminton with Vlad at the leisure centre in Stamford Road; on Wednesday he was there again, swimming with Kenneth and a brother or two, and then hung around at home until it was time for football practice.

He would have cycled down to Riverside, but his rear light was looking feeble and Ingrid, as predicted, said that she did not care for him travelling the ring road, even on the cycle path, after dark; but even so, getting down there on the bus was no problem. Coming from a place where public transport stopped at six-thirty, he was still vaguely surprised to find that he could catch a bus to the stop at the end of the road as late as midnight, should he need to; that at any time of day he could be in the city centre within ten minutes.

As the bus left the main streets he tried to chart the route for future reference, since he intended

to wear down Ingrid's resistance to his cycling –
he would soon be taller than her anyway, which
would give him an advantage – but once away
from the houses, on uninhabited roads between
hedges, he lost track of their progress. The occasional passenger who rang the bell and got off
plunged straight into anonymous unlit gloom. The
vapour that was rising off the river tonight was
fog, not mist, and visibility at ground level was
down to the width of the road when the bus
stopped and the driver called out, 'Sports
Centre'.

As soon as the vehicle moved away he could
see the sports hall silhouetted against the floodlit
fog. Lloyd wound his way through the car park –
there were many fewer cars in it this week – and
drew the neck of his sweater up over his nose
and mouth to keep out the flavour of the fog;
industrial fog, tasting of metal and toxic com-
pounds. It was not all that far to the entrance from
the bus stop, but he was consoled to know he
would not be making the reverse journey in three
hours' time; glad to be able to look forward to the
promised lift in Keith's father's car.

He did hope Keith would be there; no Keith, no
lift, but there was more to it than that. There
would be no Fred to show him around tonight; he
would have to go in on his own. Since last week
he had carried the picture in the back of his mind
of Keith being there in the changing room before
him, waving a welcome as he came through the
door. If Keith were not there, ill perhaps, or
delayed, he would have to start all over again; it
wasn't that he *needed* someone to pair off with,
but it would make such a difference to be able to
walk straight up to a friend instead of having to

plough through cohorts of cousins, brothers, old mates who had been around since play school. Last week it had not mattered that no one spoke to him because he had been a stranger. If no one spoke to him this week it would be because no one had anything to say to him. Lloyd went in through the double glass doors and down the corridor to the changing rooms very slowly.

He was among the first to arrive this time and Keith was not one of the half dozen half-dressed people in the changing room, but before disappointment could get to work and draw him down, someone behind him called, 'Hey! Lloyd!' He turned, and there was Keith, beaming and bowed down under his sports bag, which he balanced on his shoulder. COLUMBUS grinned across his sweatshirt.

'Wondered if you'd be here.'

'I said I would, didn't I?' Lloyd hoped that Keith had not forgotten about the offer of a lift.

'Yes, but a lot of people only show up once; can't stand the pace, see? Dad'll pick us up at nine-thirty.' Lloyd relaxed and started to get changed. Keith was here, pleased to see him, and he would be taken home afterwards. Now he could concentrate on the evening ahead.

It turned out even better than he expected. Once again he was chosen to remain as corner-back, when all the others had to change positions, and the coach saw him off afterwards with encouraging words: 'Carry on like this and you'll be our Most Promising Young Player of the Year.'

Still thinking of this, he shouldered his way out of the sweaty crowd round the showers and went to wait for Keith by the main entrance.

100

Keith, when he emerged, was not alone. Walking beside him, and leaning on him, was a much taller boy whom, Lloyd had noticed earlier – because he was marking the yoghurt eater – in the cornerback practice. He had been thundering around with the best of them; now he was limping painfully and his face looked grey and pinched.

'Done your ankle in?' Lloyd asked with a look of true sympathy, but inwardly cursing. He had expected to have Keith to himself for a bit.

'Osgood Schlatter,' the limping boy said, obscurely. Lloyd thought he must be introducing himself.

'Lloyd Slater,' he said. 'What did you do?'

'Osgood Schlatter's Disease,' the boy said, looking at Lloyd as though he thought he must be barmy, which he very likely did. 'It's my knee.'

'A lot of young athletes have it,' Keith said, knowledgeably. 'It's the running that does it.'

'It goes off after a bit,' the boy said. 'I'm not supposed to do anything that involves running or jumping, but you can't keep missing practices.'

'Won't that make it worse, not resting it?'

'Not really – it just doesn't get better. You grow out of it in the end.'

Lloyd felt faintly inadequate, thinking of all the running and jumping that he did with impunity. Why didn't he have Osgood Schlatter's Disease – not that he actively wanted it, but even so, it hinted at dedicated professionalism.

'Here's Dad,' Keith said. 'I'll ask if he can drop you off.' He dived down the steps as a dark car drew out of the fog. Hot exhaust vaporized round its wheels until it seemed to float on a cloud of dry ice. Keith put his head in at the passenger window and then gestured with his arm. Lloyd

101

offered his shoulder to Osgood Schlatter and they limped cautiously down the wet steps.

'You go in front,' Keith said to Osgood Schlatter, 'then you can keep your leg straight.'

'Let's sort this out,' said a man's good-natured voice from the driving seat. The courtesy light was dim and Lloyd could see only the back of a head and shoulders. 'You –' the head nodded to Osgood Schlatter '– live in Felix Street, right? Not far from us. So we'll drop Lloyd first – hello Lloyd, nice to meet you – and then take you to your door, OK?'

Lloyd climbed into the back beside Keith and the car pulled away. Now he was going to be dumped before he'd had a chance to suggest that he and Keith might meet up socially before next Wednesday. For all he knew, Osgood Schlatter was one of Keith's oldest friends, dating from the time when they had first met over the sand tray in the reception class. If he issued an invitation to Keith it would sound rude unless he included Osgood. He hoped that Osgood would be too severely injured to accept; not that he had anything against him otherwise. He seemed pleasant enough.

'How are you enjoying it?' Lloyd realized that Mr Mainwaring must be addressing him, although he had not taken his eyes off the road.

'It's brilliant,' Lloyd said. This was not entirely the truth but he did not want to sound critical in front of the others, and in any case, it was getting better all the time.

'Keith says you attracted Coach's attention the first week. Pretty fast work.'

'I like playing,' Lloyd said, modestly.

'Liking's not enough. There's more to it than

that.' Lloyd felt sure that he must be glowing faintly in the dark.

'You'll have to direct me from here,' Mr Mainwaring said, when they left the ring road by the North End turn.

'Somewhere down near the park will do,' Lloyd said. 'It isn't far.'

'No, no. We'll take you to the door. It's no night to be wandering the streets.'

Lloyd agreed. The fog was now so thick he could see it writhing in the headlights. 'Turn left here, then,' he said, 'and second right, by the phone box.'

'You doing anything on Friday?' Keith said.

'I'm playing badminton in the afternoon, but –'

'Shall we meet in town in the morning? We could have a burger or something for lunch.'

'Now where?'

'Third left, by the off-licence.'

Mr Mainwaring was not driving fast, but half-way down Aston Road he had to brake sharply as three figures hustled across the road in front of him.

'All OK in the back?' he said. 'Damn thing's stalled. Your knee all right, lad? Silly young fools – they don't show up at the best of times.'

The three youths, who had already been swallowed up in the fog, had been wearing dark blue parkas. 'No,' Lloyd said, still shaken up by the sudden jolt. 'You can see why they tell you to wear something white at night.'

'Particularly those of the Asian persuasion,' Mr Mainwaring said, and chuckled softly. Lloyd, who thought that one of the boys had been Imran, did not immediately take in what he meant.

'You're right in the middle of our ethnic community here, aren't you?' Mr Mainwaring said. 'Quite cosmopolitan.'

'Left here,' Lloyd said. 'That tall house where the curtains aren't drawn.'

The car pulled up. 'See you Friday,' Keith said. 'Where shall we meet?'

Lloyd stepped out on to the greasy pavement. 'Outside Boots?' He rarely went into the city and it was the only landmark he could think of on the spur of the moment. 'Ten-thirty?'

'OK. See you.'

'Thanks for the lift,' Lloyd said, to the back of Mr Mainwaring's head, as Keith tugged the door shut. The tail lights vanished eerily, as if the car had glided into a Black Hole. He stood for a moment in the street, looking up at the house; Paul's lighted window in the gable, a lamp on the sill of the living-room bay, but darkness in between. His mother was not in the study, working; they would be able to sit and talk, which would make a nice change. He ran up the steps and pushed open the front door which Ingrid had left on the latch. The hall awaited him, warm and softly lit, and as he shut the door against the fog he felt, for the first time since they moved in, that he was coming home.

'Is that you or a burglar?' Ingrid called from the kitchen.

'A burglar,' Lloyd said.

'Do you want a coffee before you do us over?'

'Please.' He was about to hang his jacket on the newel post when he noticed that someone, probably Paul, had left a canvas propped against the foot of the stairs. He moved it into the light to see it better and recognized Bianca, evidently a self-portrait, for the figure was turned slightly sideways and one arm was raised as if the hand on the end of it had been holding a paint brush. It must have been painted some time ago. Bianca did not look any younger but her hair was done in a style that had gone out of fashion; the braids were there, but each one was threaded with dozens of little ceramic beads, blue, green and white. From the way they were painted he could see that it was the beads that had interested Bianca, not her own face. The features were scarcely more than sketched in, lashes lowered over eyes, lips closed over teeth; all the light had been taken by Bianca's jewellery; the beads, the blue bangles on her lifted arm, the rings on the fingers that lay in her lap.

'Spectacular, isn't it?' Ingrid said, coming out of the kitchen with the coffee mugs.

'Are we keeping it?'

'No such luck. Paul's getting it framed for her – or for him. Wouldn't I love to buy it?' She went into the living-room and Lloyd followed. 'Did you have a good time?'

'Better than last week. They said I was the most promising young player – or I might be.'

'I hate to sound as if I'm dashing your hopes,' Ingrid said, 'but how serious are you about all this?'

'Of course I'm serious.'

'Only they showed a clip of a game this evening. Some of those fellows must weigh twenty stone.'

'Well, yes, the tackles and that. They aren't *all* that big; and a lot of it's padding.'

'It's just that I can't see you ending up as anything like twenty stone – or even fifteen. We're a fairly slight family, on both sides.'

'What about your Uncle Bertil?'

'That was obesity,' Ingrid said. 'Bertil wouldn't have got far even as a Sumo wrestler. Seriously, that game I saw, even the little ones were big – if you see what I mean? How do they decide from people your age who's likely to be worth hanging on to?'

'Imran's my age,' Lloyd said. 'You can see what he'll be like.'

'Quite, and I can see what you'll be like. Is the injury count anything like it is for Rugby? You hear awful things about paralysed schoolboys and broken necks.'

Lloyd was thinking of Imran, leaping from beneath the wheels of Mr Mainwaring's car. 'What's cosmopolitan?'

'It's a magazine. Talk about changing the subject.'

'No, what's it mean?'

'Literally, I suppose, it means that the universe is your city. You feel at home anywhere no matter what your nationality, or what language you speak.'

'Or what colour you are.'

'Yes. And if you describe a *place* as cosmopolitan, it means that anyone could feel at home in it.'

'It's a good thing to be, then.'

'Well, of course it is,' Ingrid said. 'Look at North End, look at this street, for a start. I should think we've got representatives of every race and nationality on earth between here and Stamford Road; that's cosmopolitan if you like; everyone shaking down well together. Why do you ask? Did you use it the wrong way?'

'Use what the wrong way?'

106

'The word – cosmopolitan. Did you think it meant something different?'

'No, I just heard somebody . . .' Mr Mainwaring had not sounded as though he were using the word as a compliment. After the near miss in Aston Road, everything he had said seemed to have a dull sound to it, like a note rung on a cracked bell. 'Those of the Asian persuasion,' he had said and at the time Lloyd had appreciated the chime of it, but it had been off-key, nasty-minded almost, the notion that Imran and his friends hadn't shown up in the dark because they were dark skinned. It might have been better, he thought, if Mr Mainwaring had wound down the window and bawled them out for being such silly sods as to step off the pavement without looking, in fact anything would have been better than that snide, soft little joke.

On the way up to bed he paused again at the foot of the stairs to look at the portrait. Now that he studied it more closely he saw that Bianca hadn't really painted herself into the background at all. The light fell on the broad slope of her nose, her cheekbone, on the curve of her lower lip. What would Mr Mainwaring have said had he met Bianca in the dark? And what would Lloyd have done about it?'

What Lloyd had hoped for, coming home in the car, was a moment to discuss with Keith exactly what they were going to do on Friday. On the couple of occasions he had gone into town with James Christopher they had toured the bicycle shops, of which there were several, probably because the Polytechnic students had so far to travel between sites. It was for the students'

107

benefit, no doubt, that they had such pretentious names; *Cyclomania*, *Velocipedia*, *Cyclopedia*, *Cyclops*, this last having a huge painted eye on a bracket over the door. Lloyd could spend many happy hours cruising from shop to shop, but Keith had not expressed any interest in cycling nor, come to that, in any of the other things which Lloyd might have shared with him. As he walked into town on Friday morning he began to doubt that they had anything in common except the gridiron, but then, he had nothing much in common with anyone, apart from the sports they played. He couldn't imagine sitting down with any of them and having the kind of conversation he had enjoyed with Ingrid and Paul and Bianca on Sunday. With the others, it was all technicalities and jokes. How would they keep going without the jokes?

And what had he ever talked about with Stephen and David and Frizzo? He could not really remember any of them *talking* to each other, it had all been climbing about, swinging from things, yelling, kicking, chucking, hooting. Now he came to think about it, they might just as well have been four chimpanzees dressed up in jeans to advertise tea bags.

Keith was propped against the plate glass window of Boots, eating crisps. When Lloyd came up to him he held out the bag, hospitably offering the last crisp.

'What are we going to do, then?' Lloyd asked, baldly.

'How long have you got?'

'I'm meeting Vlad at two-thirty. I don't have to go home first.'

'We could go down the museum,' Keith suggested. 'It's great down there.'

'Down where? I didn't know we had a museum here.'

'Everywhere's got a museum,' Keith said. 'It's underneath City Hall. I've got this history work to do for school, about what the city was like during the war. They've got this map down there, showing where all the bombs fell, and that. And they've got all these pamphlets too. Trouble is, everyone else will do it. We always end up everybody doing the same research. They ought to give us all something different. Don't you think the teachers must get bored reading it all?'

'They expect to be,' Lloyd said, 'or they'd do something about it. It's probably in their job descriptions.'

They set off down the High Street toward City Hall, which stood at an intersection. Built in more confident times, it reared up above the surrounding shops, grey stone walls with Gothic windows, battlements and pinnacles, so that it looked as if it had been planned as a cathedral, only hostilities had broken out half-way through. Beside it, the modern block which housed the Register Office and the DHSS resembled a small nuclear power station.

'Wouldn't it be better – well, different –' Lloyd said, 'to talk to somebody who remembers the place during the war? Haven't you got any ancient neighbours?'

'Not living nearby,' Keith said. 'They're mostly people like us – except the Kumaris at the Post Office. *They* weren't here during the war.'

The DHSS was doing better trade than the Register Office, and the steps going up to the entrance were crowded. There was a ramp for prams and wheelchairs, but two skinheads, with regulation cans of lager, had parked themselves across it with outstretched legs, daring anyone to try and get past them or run them over. As far as Lloyd knew, they were the only skinheads in town; he had never noticed many about the place, but even two were enough to cause an obstruction. As they had doubtless forecast, no one cared to risk asking them to move, and coming down the steps, with an overloaded buggy, was Mrs Hussain, huddled into a bulky woollen coat that made her seem smaller than ever. Lloyd ran up the steps and lifted the buggy by the front wheels. Laden with carrier bags and the infant Hussain, who blew a friendly bubble at him, it was surprisingly heavy, but he was rather less surprised than Mrs Hussain, who clearly thought for a moment that she was being attacked. Her eyes widened with alarm.

'It's me!' Lloyd cried. 'You know – next door but one. The Slaters.'

She recognized him then and smiled, as they staggered down the steps together. The baby – Lloyd did not know its name or whether it was a boy or a girl – regarded him genially from its pillow and grabbed his sleeve as if it needed to tell him something urgently.

'Thank you,' Mrs Hussain murmured, eyes cast down again, and launched the buggy into the surging crowds, fragile but determined. Lloyd thought her feet looked dreadfully cold in their open-work sandals, in spite of the heavy coat.

'You know her?' Keith said, curiously.

'Neighbours,' Lloyd said. 'Mrs Hussain. I don't know what the baby's called.'

'That's the real difference,' Keith said, as they turned toward City Hall, 'during the war there weren't any of *them*.'

'What, skinheads?'

'No.' Keith jerked his head in the direction of Mrs Hussain's retreating back. '*Them*. But you're not allowed to say that, of course.'

'No, I'm sorry,' Mrs Sutton said, in her distant telephone voice, 'Stephen's out at the moment. Shall I get him to ring you when he comes in?'

'Yes – no – it's all right,' Lloyd said. 'It wasn't important. Thank you. Goodbye.'

'Have you finished with the phone yet?' Ingrid said, over the banisters.

'Yet?'

'That must be the fifth call you've made.'

'Third. Couldn't get through the other two times. How do you know?'

'I have my methods. When you dial down here, the extension clicks upstairs. I think there ought to be a mystery novel in that. If you count the clicks you can work out which digits are being dialled. Imagine your secret agent noting down telephone numbers by listening to an extension. Who were you trying to call?'

'I thought you would have worked it out,' Lloyd said sourly.

'Not me. You have to be an expert – it's very fast.'

'I was just ringing Stephen – and Frizzo – and David. They're all out.'

'Then you won't mind going to the Co-op for me?'

'I'll go. We out of coffee again?'

'We're out of everything,' Ingrid said. 'I made a list. If anyone rings back while you're away, can I give them a message?'

'No,' Lloyd said. 'It doesn't matter. There wasn't anything to say, anyway.'

CHAPTER EIGHT

'Anyone going to the fireworks?' Vlad asked at morning break on Wednesday.

'When? Fireworks already?' It was so long since they had celebrated Bonfire Night at home Lloyd had forgotten that Guy Fawkes was due for his anniversary.

'You *can't* have forgotten,' Vlad cried. 'It's one of those great autumn festivals; folklore, primitive rites – like Hallowe'en, the Miss World Contest.'

'You don't have Guy Fawkes in the Ukraine, do you?' Kenneth said.

'We're picking up your customs. I've never *been* to the Ukraine. Even Dad can hardly remember it,' Vlad said.

'You can't call Guy Fawkes a *primitive* rite, he tried to blow up Parliament in 1605.'

'Miss World's primitive.' Lloyd was abashed

that Chinese Kenneth should know more English history than he did. 'Do they have a firework display here?'

'In Stamford Park – down in the town, Friday night,' Vlad said. 'Let's all go – get up a party.'

'What d'you mean, all?' Kenneth said. 'All three of us?'

'We could ask some of the others as well. Do you think Zoe . . .?'

'She doesn't go around with the likes of us,' Lloyd said. 'She thinks we're Ists. What about Salman?'

'Not on a Friday,' Kenneth said. 'Anyway, he doesn't go to anything like that.'

'We could ask James,' Lloyd said, 'and I've got this friend down at American football. He might.'

'Not the one from Highbridge?' Kenneth said. 'Would *he* go round with the likes of us?'

Lloyd thought about that on the way home. Since Friday he had been thinking a great deal about what Keith might say when and if he met the rest of Lloyd's friends. He surely wouldn't be so tactless as to say anything in front of Salman or Imran, but when you got down to it, it was hardly a matter of tact. Being tactful made no difference to what he actually thought, although Lloyd had spent five days trying to persuade himself that Keith was being genuinely thoughtless, literally didn't think, was just parroting the remarks he must have grown up hearing his father make. The real problem, Lloyd realized, with both Keith and his father, was that they must assume that Lloyd felt exactly the same way; and the reason they assumed that was because he had said nothing to make it clear, or even likely, that he did not.

In which case, what had Keith thought when Lloyd had helped Mrs Hussain down the steps with her buggy? All he could remember was what Keith had said afterwards: 'They're always down the DHSS. They only come over here for the dole.' Lloyd, who had supposed that Mrs Hussain was there on account of Child Benefit, had not known where to start arguing. Mr Hussain had his own business – his name was on the side of the van, Salman's father was a teacher, Imran's a bus driver. Anwar's uncle, with whom he lived, ran a delicatessen. And every mother in the country was entitled to Child Benefit, even Princess Diana, probably.

'You gone to sleep?' asked James, who was riding beside him.

'I often sleep all the way home,' Lloyd said. 'My bike knows the way. It just stops at the front gate.'

'Oh, yeah?' James said. 'How come you've missed your turning, then?'

Lloyd saw that without noticing he had cycled all the way to the end of Aston Road, and it was outside James's front gate that they had stopped. He smacked his bicycle reprovingly over the lamp bracket. 'Oh well, it often comes down here on its own. It's got a friend at the fish shop.'

He hoped that now they had reached James's house James might invite him in. He wanted someone to talk to, but James made no move to issue an invitation and, he recalled, he wasn't sure what kind of a reception his dilemma would get from James. James did not like Salman because Salman was so abrasive; at least, that was the reason James had given . . .

'I know what I meant to ask you,' he said, as he

turned the bicycle, 'some of us are going down to the fireworks on Friday. Do you want to come?'

'Who?' James said at once.

'Me and Kenneth and Vlad, so far,' Lloyd said. 'We thought we'd eat at The Pizza Place first and get properly warm, and then go on to the display in Stamford Park. And Salman might come,' he added, knowing quite well that Salman would not.

'I'll let you know,' James said. 'I think we're going out on Friday night. See you.' He wheeled his bicycle down the alley beside his house and left Lloyd at the kerb, none the wiser and just as uneasy as before.

'Same arrangement as last week?' Ingrid asked as he came downstairs with his kit. 'You'll get a lift home?'

'That's right,' Lloyd said. 'I'll be back by ten.'

'Cheer up. You're not having second thoughts, are you?' Ingrid said.

'What about?'

'The football. The first two weeks you couldn't wait to get down there. Last time you must have arrived half an hour early. Now look at you – it's ten past six already.'

'There's no point in getting there too soon,' Lloyd said. 'And it doesn't matter if I miss some of the warm-up session.'

'You've certainly changed your tune. When I wanted you to clear up in the kitchen before you left it was absolutely vital that you were there for every second of it.'

'I *have* cleared up in the kitchen,' Lloyd said, pointedly, as he had not been asked to do it, this time. He slung his sports bag over his shoulder and went out down the front steps. There was no fog now, the night was clear and a half moon hung between the houses. He did not want to be late, to miss the warm-up session, but his pleasure in the evening had been poisoned by the prospect of the way it might end in the car, with Keith or his father saying things that he did not want to hear.

When he arrived Keith was already changed and out on the field, jogging. Lloyd waited until he was on the far side before joining the runners, so that there was little chance of either one catching up with the other; and if Keith accelerated or dropped back, Lloyd could see and would be able to do likewise.

They did not really meet until it was time for position practice. Lloyd found himself called to be a cornerback yet again, which was all very well in its way, but he would have liked a chance to try something else. Was he never going to get a turn in an attacking formation; wide receiver, quarterback, man in motion, even, ready to take up any position? Perhaps the coach could already see that he would never make a tackle. None of Great-Uncle Bertil's legendary poundage had come down to him.

'Didn't think you were here,' Keith said, when it was his turn as wide receiver with Lloyd.

'Missed the bus,' Lloyd said, as the ball came toward him and they took off. The conversation proceeded at widely spaced intervals as the players changed places.

'You doing anything Friday night?'

'Might be, why?'

'What about Friday, then?'

'There's a whole bunch of us from school going to the fireworks.'

'Which fireworks?'

'I said, which fireworks?'

'Stamford Park. You want to come?'

'We usually go over to –'

'I don't know about Friday. We usually go over to friends. They have a proper bonfire party and a barbecue.'

'You want to come with us instead?'

'I'll see what Dad says.'

Lloyd managed to get a shower before Keith was even undressed. Afterwards he escaped from the steamy mass as fast as he could and went to wait by the main entrance. As he stood there, watching his reflection in the dark glass of the doors, and deciding that he must measure himself again when he got home, a familiar figure came down the corridor to his left, swinging a racquet.

'Anwar!'

Anwar nodded amiably as if they were old friends. In white sports shirt and shorts The Man Most Likely looked more likely than ever; tall, suave, athletic and indecently grown-up. Anwar's moustache had come on a treat over half term. He slapped the racquet against his hairy calf.

'What are you doing here?'

'I've been playing squash.'

'Do you come here often?'

'Two or three times a week,' Anwar said. 'How come I never saw you before?'

'I've only been three times. I play American football.'

'Do you really?' Anwar looked interested. 'I thought that was one of those things everybody talked about and nobody did. Like sex,' he added, casually.

'We don't really play – but we're preparing for it,' Lloyd said. He could hardly believe that he was standing here, chatting to The Man Most Likely, the nearest thing to God in the Third Year.

'Don't you have to weigh two hundred pounds and train with lead in your boots, or something? I thought you played badminton.'

'Well I do, but I've always wanted to try this.' Lloyd was amazed that Anwar should know about the badminton. 'I mean, I play cricket, too, and swim.'

'You're all over the place, aren't you?' Anwar flashed his fabulous smile. 'Man in motion. See you.' He raised his racquet in graceful salute and strode toward the changing rooms. At the door he tangled with someone coming out. There was much bowing and scraping and fast footwork before Anwar managed to step aside and hold open the door, in such a way that the person on the other side had to duck under his arm. It was Keith. He dodged round Anwar without saying anything, but turned and gave him a hard look as he passed serenely into the changing room.

'They're all over the place,' he said. Lloyd could feel nothing but relief when Mr Mainwaring arrived with the car and said that he thought the Brothertons would be hurt if Keith did not go to their firework party.

In the end, Lloyd's own firework party was just himself and Vlad. At the last moment Kenneth was descended upon by relatives.

'Sorry,' he said, breaking the news at lunch-time on Friday, but he did not look particularly grieved.

'They won't miss you for a couple of hours,' Vlad said.

'But I don't want to miss *them*,' Kenneth protested. 'It's my auntie and uncle from Manchester – and my cousins.'

'What, the ones who came swimming with us?' Lloyd said. 'You only saw them a few weeks ago.'

'No, not them. Anyway, if it *was* them I'd still want to see them.'

'I'd go a long way to miss seeing my cousins,' Lloyd said.

'I don't know,' Salman said; 'how does a country full of people who don't want to see each other end up with a population of sixty million?'

'We run into each other occasionally,' Vlad said. 'Accidents will happen, especially in an island this size.'

'I suppose you get married by accident too,' Salman said, over his shoulder, as he and Kenneth sauntered in the direction of the canteen. 'No wonder you spend the rest of your lives avoiding each other.'

'Do you think he puts his teeth to soak in vine-gar overnight?' Vlad inquired.

'He doesn't approve of families not staying to-gether,' Lloyd said. 'His grandparents live with them, and his uncle.'

'There's so many things he doesn't approve of,' Vlad sighed. 'Do you think *he'll* have an arranged marriage?'

'Don't ask him,' Lloyd begged. 'He'll start quoting our divorce figures or something. I mean, that's what people always want to know, isn't it?

That's all anyone thinks of – arranged mar-
riages. That was all I knew about Islam till I
came here. There weren't any Muslims where I
lived before, well, not any Asians at all. We did
comparative religion in RE, but it wasn't really
that. It was comparative Christianity really, and
the Catholics spent all their time arguing with
the Church of England people. It was just like
Isms. Nobody ever took any notice of what
anyone else thought.'

'What about if you weren't anything at all?'

'Most of us weren't anything at all, but if you
said you were an atheist the teacher got ratty and
said you were too young to know.'

'I've noticed that,' Vlad said. 'Nobody ever
tells you you're too young to know if you're a
Christian.'

'What about Muslims?'

'I think you're just born one. If your parents
are, you are, Salman says.'

'Anwar?'

Vlad considered. 'He doesn't look too worried,
does he?'

'Are you a Catholic?'

'I suppose we'd be Eastern Orthodox if we
were anything,' Vlad said, 'only we aren't. You
know, priests with beards and onions on the roof.
I think my cousins are.'

'Not you as well,' Lloyd moaned.

'Calm down,' Vlad said. 'They won't be turning
up this evening, they're in Kiev. Lloyd, are your
parents divorced?'

'Yes,' Lloyd said. 'Why?'

'You never mention your father. I think mine
are going to be.' Lloyd looked at Vlad and saw
all at once that his pale and sinister expression

121

was really one of great sadness. Vlad shrugged and changed the subject abruptly. 'Let's go to the canteen before all the chips get eaten by the heathen hordes.'

'What is a heathen, exactly?' Lloyd said, following him.

'Anybody who doesn't believe in what you believe in,' Vlad said, 'which is just about everyone.'

'Better to be a heathen than an Ist,' Lloyd said.

He had never been into Stamford Park before, but he had often passed the gates. They were imposing wrought iron constructions bearing the corporation coat of arms on gilded shields, hung between massive stone posts. As far as the eye could see beyond them, lay formal flower beds, shrubberies, avenues of trees. It made Victoria Park look like a back garden and seemed an unlikely setting for the black and sulphurous excesses of a firework display, but once past the conifer walks, the terrain became very different. There were seven or eight acres at least of grass, then more trees, and after that the park reverted to what it must have been to begin with, a marshy meadow bounded by thorn hedges. In the darkness Lloyd was having to guess at all this, but he knew a field when he found one, and a thorn, when it found him. He and Vlad had arrived early and taken up prime positions just behind the rope barricade, next to the hedge which grabbed at their garments hungrily, with talons. The fireworks blazed and blinded, leaving him with green and scarlet bomb bursts behind his eyelids, but after the fireworks came the bonfire, a roaring pyramid of flame, and Lloyd saw that he had been right about the field, the leafless hedges, the tussocks of grass, the miry depressions in one of which he and Vlad were standing.

'No wonder my feet are so cold,' Vlad said, looking down at the water which he could now see oozing over the welts of his shoes. 'See what I mean about primitive rites?'

Lloyd looked back down the crescent of gaping faces that curved away along the line of the barrier.

'I bet that's how people behaved at human sacrifices,' Vlad said. 'In fact, I bet that if that was a real person up there now instead of a Guy, they'd all go on cheering. You know how crowds turn into mobs. Shall we go now?'

'In a minute. Wait till the fire dies down a bit.'

'OK, but let's get away before everyone else makes a move. It wouldn't take much to turn this lot into a mob.'

'Come off it,' Lloyd said, 'they're just having a good time.'

'People who went witch-hunting were having a good time. I expect the Nazis were having a good time.'

'It was you that wanted to come.'

'Yes, sorry; I just don't like crowds,' Vlad said. Lloyd noticed that in spite of having agreed to stay until the fire died down, Vlad was sidling away along the hedge, almost as if he were being dragged and had no choice. 'I always came with Mum and Dad before; you know, when you're little you feel safe so long as you're with Mum and Dad.'

'What do you mean, when you were little?' Lloyd said. 'Last year?'

'No, we didn't come last year. There was some row going on at home and they wouldn't let me come on my own. This time I just said I was going and nobody said I couldn't. Don't think I'll do it again, though. Awful, isn't it,' Vlad said, unfathomable in the darkness, 'how much you change in two years.'

Underfoot the ground became firmer, the grass flatter, and their shadows, cast before them by the fire at their backs, stretched out trembling on the cropped turf of the park proper. Then the crinoline skirts of the conifers closed behind them and the fire was no more than a distant crackle.

'What's the time?' Vlad said.

'Nearly nine. It's a pity we had that pizza first, we could have done with it now.'

'Sort of supper after the theatre,' Vlad said. 'I haven't got enough money left for another one, have you?'

'We could get some chips.'

'Yes, but then I'll have to go home. I said I'd be in by half past.'

'Doesn't that mean ten? When I say I'll be in by a certain time Ingrid knows I'll be half an hour late. It's a sort of code.'

'Not in our house. Half past means half past or it's Spanish Inquisition time.'

'Do you go to the theatre much?'

'Used to, all the time,' Vlad said. 'We went to London every month, specially, and Stratford in the summer, and there's often something on down the road – the Theatre Royal. You get a lot of Shakespeare there.'

'Do you like Shakespeare?'

'He's brilliant,' Vlad said. 'He's so funny. Even *Hamlet*'s funny in places. You know, the gravedigger, working out how long a body's been in the ground by the moisture content.'

Lloyd knew that he was going to show up badly in this conversation. Ingrid was no theatre-goer and apart from occasional glimpses on television, he had never seen any Shakespeare. Then he was inspired.

'Why does Hamlet have a skull?'

'He didn't *have* it – not to carry around with him. He picks it up in the graveyard. It's the same scene; the gravedigger asks him if he knows whose skull it was, and it turns out to be someone he knew.'

'Yorick.'

'That's right.' Vlad looked delighted and Lloyd felt it.

'Is that one of the funny bits?'

'Well, no; I mean, you think how you'd feel if it happened to you – the shock. *The Comedy of Errors* is my favourite, though,' he went on, sounding really happy, for once. 'That's got to be the funniest play *ever*.'

'Which chippie shall we go to?' Lloyd said.

'Fryer Tuck does the best chips round here,' Vlad said, 'and it's half-way between yours and mine. Let's go there. Tell you what,' he said, suddenly, 'they're doing *Twelfth Night* at the Theatre Royal after Christmas. Shall we go?'

'To the theatre?'

'Why not? Just us, we won't try and get up a party. They'll all get an attack of cousins at the last moment. Shall we?'

'Well . . . yes,' Lloyd said, uncertainly.

'Don't you like Shakespeare?'

'Of course I do.' Lloyd swore on the instant to make it come true. 'I just don't know *Twelfth Night*.'

'Brilliant,' Vlad said confidently. 'You'll love it. I'll get Mum to book for us tomorrow.'

If it had not been for the creaking floorboards up above, Lloyd would have forgotten for long stretches that Paul lived in the house. He was so very quiet, although traces of him appeared briefly, a carrier bag on the landing, boots left drying by the back door. Bianca's portrait turned up again in the hall, cleverly framed in narrow bands of black wood that made you see how much light there was in the picture.

'Is she coming to collect it?' Lloyd asked hopefully, when he found Paul in the kitchen, making coffee.

'No, I'm taking it down to Dover on Friday night,' Paul said. 'She wants it for an exhibition.'

'She's not going to sell it, is she?'

'If anyone wants to buy.'

'Don't you want it?' He hated the thought of Bianca going to strangers.

'Of course I want it, but the way the mortgage rate is going we need every penny we can scrape together. And that should fetch three hundred.'

'Pennies?'

'Don't look so shocked,' Paul said. 'She's a professional. What she paints, she sells. She's not so successful yet that she can turn down an offer and keep a work if someone wants to buy. Not like my water-colour class.'

'What, Fred and them? Is that where you've been tonight?'

'Alas. Hard to imagine Fred painting in water-colour.' Paul smiled. 'But he's not bad. He knows it's an odd thing for a big bloke like him to be doing so he takes it a lot more seriously than some of the others. He doesn't just want to produce pretty pictures.' Paul stirred his coffee and began to carry it away. 'You must admit,' he said, 'that Fred has wide interests.'

'Water-colour and football.'

'Very rare bird, our Fred.'

At the mention of American football the discomfort that Lloyd had been trying to suppress all week came looming up again. He had more or less made up his mind that he would not go to the practice on Wednesday. That would give him time to think, as if he had not had time enough already, how he was going to deal with Keith and Keith's father. The more they saw of him, the more they said and he failed to challenge, the more they would assume he agreed with them. At one point he had come up with the dramatic idea of inviting Keith to Victoria Park one Sunday to play cricket, so that Keith would see, without being told, who Lloyd's other friends were, but Keith had never talked about cricket; and you would have to be a real maniac like Imran or Salman to want to play it in November. Well, then, what about the indoor nets on Saturday mornings? More than half the boys who attended were Asian; but supposing Keith began making his remarks there, where everyone could hear him and know that he was making them to Lloyd. What would Lloyd do then, and how would he be received the next time he went to the nets? Tomorrow, he decided, as he watched Paul carry Bianca's portrait upstairs, he would stay at home and tell Ingrid that he had too much homework. That would please her, the thought that he was putting school before sport, and he would come out of the affair with some credit at least.

He was right about that. Ingrid was so impressed by his devotion to duty that she almost urged him to go to American football instead. He sat up in his bedroom, which overlooked the back garden, and worked assiduously all evening, getting so much done that he found, when Ingrid called him down for dinner at nine, that he was not only up to date with his assignments, but had made inroads into the work scheduled for next week.

Overhead he heard the occasional creak as Paul crossed the attic room, and his footsteps descending the stairs when he came down to the loo, but otherwise the house was silent. Ingrid, having put a casserole in the oven, returned to her study to work, but she was not typing this evening.

Lloyd stared out of the window, over the black bosky garden, faintly illuminated by other people's windows. The fog, which had returned, as it always does on November 6th, fed by the smoke of the night before, was thinning again, and hung about, trapped by trees and bushes. Down at Riverside, under the floodlights, he knew that at this moment they would be engaged in practice for positions, and there would be one cornerback missing. Had he been missed? Keith would notice he was not there. It suddenly struck him that Keith might ring up, tomorrow, and ask where he had been. Too much homework, he would say again. No one ever argued with that.

Keith rang next day.

'What happened to you on Wednesday?' he asked, cheerfully.

Now was the moment to tell him but Lloyd, caught on the hop, could not find the words. Keith sounded so innocent.

'Too much homework,' he said. 'I had this assignment to hand in – you know how it gets left till the last moment.'

'Coach wondered where you were. You're coming next week, aren't you?'

'I hope so,' Lloyd said.

'What are you doing on Saturday?'

'Cricket.' Should he invite Keith along to meet the others? 'Only I don't know if I can make that, even. I did my knee in playing badminton after school.'

'How? You twist it?'

'No, I came down too heavily on one foot. I've got a support on it. I might have to go to the doctor's, it really is swollen.'

'You ought to rest it, then. Let me know how it is, then I can tell Coach.'

'OK, thanks for ringing. See you.'

Lloyd put down the receiver. Keith was so nice, so thoughtful. He might even call round to see how Lloyd was. He couldn't imagine anyone else doing that. On the other hand, he couldn't think of anyone else he would want to discourage from coming.

CHAPTER NINE

On the way to SAS on Friday, Mr Moran cornered him in the corridor.

'Slater! It *is* Slater, isn't it?' Lloyd felt like replying, 'Yes, Mr Moran – it *is* Mr Moran, isn't it?' but guessed that this would not go down too well, and it was additionally unfair. There were only five PE teachers whose names had to be memorized, and more than eight hundred students.

'I hear from Vladimov that you play badminton at least as well as he does. Is that right?'

Lloyd could imagine Vlad saying that, without at all meaning to boast, but he was surprised to hear it coming back to him via Mr Moran.

'We play together out of school, Sir,' he said.

'Why not in school?'

'The seniors have always got the courts,' Lloyd said.

'But what about the badminton club?'

'Bit of a shambles, isn't it, Sir?' He saw Mr Moran's eyebrows go up. 'No – not a shambles exactly, but about half the people who go just muck around. I mean, they take up all the room and the ones who really want to play have to do doubles and there's only time to go to seven points. You never get the chance to find out if you can play well.'

'Let's just say it's a little oversubscribed and leave it at that. We need more players your age to represent the school. Interested?'

'I might not be good enough –'

'What an enthusiastic response,' Mr Moran said. 'Can't you take Vladimov's word for it? I got the impression from him that you are a serious player.'

'I *am* serious, Sir. I just don't want to make a fool of myself at competition level.'

'I didn't say you'd been chosen sight unseen. Come along after school on Monday and we'll see if Vladimov is right. A small select group play then, including him. I think you'll find it less of a shambles. He'll give you the details.'

Lloyd wondered a little, feeling offended that Vlad had never mentioned the small select group to him; then understood his tact in *not* mentioning it until he had made arrangements for Lloyd to be invited to join. He wished there were something he could do for Vlad in return, something to cheer him up. The circles under Vlad's eyes, and the droop of his mouth, could no longer be attributed to his having been up all night looking for jugulars.

He found the SAS lesson coming to the boil when he reached the classroom. An indignant debate was already in progress and his late arrival went almost unnoticed. Mrs Baird simply waved to him and he sat down beside Vlad under cover of one of Zoe De La Hoyde's speeches.

Hearing snatches of what she said he remembered that at the end of the lesson before half term, they had been required to look out for examples of racism, one more Ism to fill in a blank patch on Friday's timetable. And he had his example now, hadn't he? He couldn't think of anything he wanted to discuss less, in public. No one would dispute that it was an example, but that would demote it to the level of a piece of school work; a piece of school work that no one took very seriously, of no more relevance than a paragraph snipped out of a newspaper and brought in for dissection by the likes of Zoe De La Hoyde, while he and James and the others tried to get on with their maths.

In fact, the subject under discussion was exactly that, a cutting from a daily paper about an arson attack in south London; a house gutted, a young mother and her three little children killed. Zoe was passionately upset, as though she had known the people concerned, and the rest of the group seemed to be with her, not surprisingly. Lloyd did not suppose that any of them would creep out by night to pour petrol through a letter-box and burn a family to death, but then, he couldn't see Keith doing it, either. Keith's particular brand of prejudice was more subtle; it did not show at first, he did not act upon it. Did they have scenes like this at Keith's school, socially aware discussions; and what did Keith do if people like Zoe stood up and made furious denunciations? The uniforms at Highbridge were distinctive, often seen about town – although not at this end of it – and now that Lloyd came to think about it, the people who wore them all seemed to be white.

Come to think about it, most of this lot were white, too. Anwar, who commanded nothing but respect, tempered by naked envy, and Salman who commanded a certain amount of fear as well, were in a different group. Vlad, noticing that Lloyd was looking round, nudged him in the arm with his pen and he turned his eyes toward the table behind him. Unobserved, Farida and Farzana were sitting silently, heads bent, holding hands. Beyond them, Kenneth, who might have been expected to declare an interest, sat hunched and oblivious, engrossed in his maths homework.

'You wouldn't care to accompany me to town, would you?' Ingrid said at breakfast time, on Saturday. No one really considered breakfast to be a meal; things were eaten as people passed through the kitchen, which was where Lloyd and Ingrid met, Lloyd going in and Ingrid coming out.

'When?' Lloyd said.

'Clearly not this morning,' Ingrid said, 'on account of the cricket. What have you got lined up for this afternoon; swimming, badminton, gridiron, tiddlywinks . . .?'

Lloyd thought furiously. He had realized, after Keith had rung up, that if he were supposed to be laid up with a bad knee, he could hardly allow himself to be seen hurtling about at the indoor cricket nets. He knew very few of the others personally, but it was quite possible that among them there might be someone who knew Keith;

not likely, but possible. Some of them might go to Highbridge – they came from schools all over the city. Feeling hunted he decided that he would give cricket the go-by this week, and had fully intended to do something demonstratively non-sexist at home; vacuum the stairs, perhaps, or clean the kitchen floor.

And if he went into town with Ingrid, he might actually run into Keith.

'Well?' Ingrid said.

'Is it shopping?'

'I could do with a hand.'

'I'll go up to the Co-op for you,' Lloyd said. 'I'm not going to the nets this week. I could go now.'

'It wasn't only that. I thought you said you needed some more trainers, for badminton, you *said*, though God knows, you need them anyway. That pair is an affront to public decency.'

'I could go in after school next week, couldn't I, if you gave me the money?'

'If I pay, I want to see what I'm paying for. I'm not shelling out an extra tenner for a fancy label with a reptile on it. Anyway, if you're not going to cricket you can come with me now.'

Arguing would be dangerous policy, he could see, and ungrateful. He did need new trainers urgently, with Monday's special badminton game coming up, and he knew that Ingrid would buy him a good pair.

'All right. Thanks. Have I got time for some corn-flakes?'

'As it's an hour till the shops open I should think you might – what have you done to your-self?' Ingrid said, as Lloyd limped past her.

'I twisted my knee.'

'When?'

'Just now, coming downstairs.'

'You look as though you've dislocated your hip,' Ingrid said, unsympathetically. Lloyd, who had paused to speak to her, tried to remember which leg he had been favouring, but Ingrid was already away down the hall. He decided on the left. It seemed to come more naturally, that side, and with a bit of rehearsal he should have quite an authentic limp by the time they got into town.

He managed to keep it up all morning, so successfully that Ingrid asked if he wouldn't like to go back on the bus as soon as they had bought the trainers, while she did the rest of the shopping. He had to refuse, of course, but he suffered for it. By the time they reached home he had discovered that favouring one leg gave you a fearful pain in the other, and when he got up on Sunday he had a real limp, in the right leg, and after all that, he had not seen Keith.

'Are you sure you're fit to cycle?' Ingrid asked, next morning. 'You seem to be coming apart at the joints.'

'It's almost worn off,' Lloyd said. He had been phasing out the limp so that no questions would be asked when he proposed to stay late at school this evening.

'You still look pretty spavined,' Ingrid said. 'I take it you won't be doing anything athletic for a while. Do you want a note to get off PE?'

'No!' The very *last* thing . . . 'No, actually, I'm staying late for extra badminton tonight.'

'Badminton? With your leg dropping off?'

'It's all *right* now,' Lloyd said. 'Well, almost. Only, like I told you, Mr Moran has a special session for promising players.'

'A couple of weeks ago you were a promising American footballer.'

'I'm probably more promising at badminton,' Lloyd said. 'Anyway, I've been *asked* to come to this.'

'You're out of your tree,' Ingrid said. 'Well, if you come crawling home this evening, don't expect any sympathy. You can look forward to an arthritic old age.'

'If I've hurt my *knee* I shan't be able to *crawl*, shall I?' Lloyd muttered, wondering where all this was going to end. He foresaw a lifetime of counterfeit leg injuries, each one contributing to the next.

At school today he must be spry and springy in his step for unless he got back into the habit of distributing his weight evenly, he really would be unfit. He had yet to decide whether or not he was going to the football practice on Wednesday. If he did not, the knee excuse would do for Ingrid *and* Keith, when he next rang up. After that, he could not begin to think what he was going to do.

He was faced with an even worse dilemma by the end of the afternoon. The badminton group, as Mr Moran had promised, was small and select. Lloyd played first with Vlad and then with Mr Moran himself, who was unexpectedly light on his feet and thrashed him. By the end of the game Lloyd saw his prospects of playing for the school in ruins. His knees began to ache in earnest, weak with disappointment, but as he was helping Vlad to dismantle the net, Mr Moran came over to them, ursine and flat of foot again.

'How do you feel –?'

'Hopeless,' Lloyd said quickly, before he could be told that he was hopeless.

'How do you feel about playing for the team on Friday?'

'But I lost,' Lloyd said. 'You wiped the floor with me.'

'Yes, but Vladimov didn't. You'll be playing against people your own age, not hardened cases at national level.'

'Did you play for England?'

'Northern Ireland,' Mr Moran said. 'How do you feel about it?'

'Yes, please,' Lloyd said. Vlad, draped like a sea nymph in the net, slapped him between the shoulders. 'We'll slay them. Who are we playing, Sir?'

'Highbridge,' Mr Moran said.

He had been home for only ten minutes on Wednesday when the telephone rang. He was in the kitchen, making coffee, but before he could run into the hall the ringing stopped as Ingrid picked up the extension in the study. Then he heard a door open upstairs. 'It's for you!'

He lifted the handset and heard the clatter as Ingrid hung up.

'Hullo?'

'It's me, Keith. Are you going tonight?'

'I can't.'

'Your knee?'

'Yes. It might be what that other guy had – Osgood Schlatter's Disease.'

Lloyd was aware of the front door opening and Paul coming in.

'What?'

'Osgood Schlatter's Disease.' The perfect alibi. Then he thought of Friday. 'I mean, it depends what I'm doing. I'm probably all right playing badminton, but anything really heavy, with a lot of running . . . you know . . .'

'Hard luck,' Keith said.

And then, as Paul closed the door, he noticed that he had Fred with him. He hoped that they would go upstairs straight away but Fred set down a large cardboard box and they were both rooting through it like kids at a bran tub.

'I'll be seeing the doctor, I expect.' Lloyd lowered his voice, prudently.

'What? I can't hear you.'

'The doctor. I'll go to the doctor about it. I'll let you know how I get on. Thanks for ringing.'

'That's OK. See you soon.'

He hung up.

'Who's seeing the doctor?' Paul said. He and Fred were on the stairs now, looking down at him. 'You? I noticed you had a gammy leg, but I thought you were over that.'

'Well . . . I'm not sure . . . you know . . . I mean . . .'

'Aren't you going to the practice tonight, then?' Fred asked. Lloyd had not bargained for Fred being there.

'I don't think so.'

'You missed last week, didn't you?'

'I had a lot of homework. How did you know?'

'Coach mentioned it. He knew I brought you along the first time. He says you're very promising, but you won't make much headway if you don't turn out regularly.' Fred did not seem very sympathetic, either. 'Did I hear you saying something about Osgood Schlatter's Disease?'

'I'm not sure, yet, but –'

'You'd better find out. I was going to suggest that you came down with me, now that I'm here, but if you can't be bothered . . .'

138

Not waiting for an answer he went on upstairs and Paul followed him. Lloyd returned to the kitchen where the kettle had boiled and switched itself off. Now big friendly Fred was annoyed with him, he was missing the practice, he might yet manoeuvre himself into missing the bad-minton match on Friday, and all through trying to do the right thing.

It was not until he had made the coffee and was carrying it upstairs to Ingrid, that there occurred to him the thought that he hadn't been trying to do the right thing at all. He had been trying not to do anything. Unlike Vlad and Salman, who in their different ways said exactly what they thought, he always opted for saying nothing.

He pushed open the study door and brought the coffee in. Ingrid reached out for it, cigarette wedged between two fingers. Lloyd had not the heart to make his customary gibe about that, even.

'Practising tonight?' Ingrid said.

'No, I don't think so.'

'Homework or knees?'

'Bit of both,' Lloyd said. He did not want to stay to talk. 'I'm going to make a start on the home-work now.'

'Noble youth,' Ingrid murmured as he went out again. 'I'm going out myself, tonight, by the way. Only for a couple of hours, but I shan't be eating here. Do you want to get fish and chips later on?'

'OK. Where are you going?'

'To borrow some tapes from a friend. I shan't be late. I'll leave the money by the phone.'

Lloyd went down the landing to his room, won-dering if Ingrid's friend were a man or a woman.

He stayed in his room until he heard Fred

going downstairs at six o'clock. He opened the bedroom window slightly and heard the car start up and drive away. A few minutes later Ingrid called up to say that she was about to leave, and then, when the front door had slammed, the house was quiet. Lloyd thought that he could do with the fish and chips right now; he had earned them, for he was shockingly ahead with his homework again.

He ran down the stairs and was swinging round the newel post toward the coins which he could see lying by the telephone, when he ran into Paul who was coming the other way, from the kitchen.

'Knees better?' Paul inquired, as they re-bounded.

'Oh, yes. It sort of comes and goes.'

'I'd noticed,' Paul said, drily. 'It's been coming and going since Friday. Are you on your way out?'

'Just to the chip shop. I don't suppose that will hurt them.'

'I shouldn't think it would. I'll drop you off there, if you like,' Paul said. 'I'm just going to look at a flat.'

'At night?'

'The owner works all day – like most of us,' Paul said. 'Do you want a lift?'

They went out into the raw evening, neither clear nor foggy but dim with clouds. 'Which chippie do you patronize?'

'There's one at the junction with Stamford Road. That'll be fine.'

When he was sitting beside Paul in the Alpine, Lloyd said, 'How's Bianca?'

'Fine. Why?'

'I thought you went down to see her at the week-end.'

140

'Yes, I did. She asked after you, actually.'

'Did she?' Lloyd felt almost cheered to think that Bianca had remembered him.

'Yes, and I said that I thought you had something on your mind.'

Lloyd sat silently and wondered how Paul had guessed. The car pulled up outside Fryer Tuck's which was, as usual, full of customers; glowing with bright lights and good humour. But he no longer wanted to go in.

'I couldn't come and see this flat with you, could I?'

'Is that your idea of an exciting evening? I don't see why not. Ingrid won't mind your being out? Did you lock up? Nothing left smouldering?'

'She's the one who leaves things smouldering. No, she won't mind. We'll be back before she is anyway, won't we?'

'I hope so. It's only a little way – just outside the ring road.' Paul started the car again. 'I take it you want to talk.'

'Yes.'

'Is this something frightful that you can't tell a respectable married woman?'

'You what?'

'Something you could have asked your father but don't want to mention to your mother.'

'Oh no, nothing like that; I just didn't know what to say to her.'

'And you know what to say to me?'

'Yes,' Lloyd said, knowing all at once that Paul would see the problem; because of Bianca. 'There's this boy I know,' he said. 'Keith Mainwaring; I met him down at American football, and we got friendly. I mean, we were friends right off, and his dad gives me a lift home afterwards. He's really friendly.'

'So far so good. What's the problem – Father?'

'No – *yes*. Probably it is. He says things, they both do.'

'What sort of things,' Paul said, sounding as if he could guess.

'Racist things. All the time, like without thinking. Every time they see somebody Asian, they say something.'

'And you, no doubt, tell them how wrong-headed they are.'

'No, I don't,' Lloyd said. 'I don't know what to say. I keep thinking they don't really mean it, especially Keith, because he's nice, really, I mean, otherwise he's nice. He rings up and asks how I am, and paid for my lunch and that. I really like him, except for what he says.'

'Is that why you've stopped going to the practices; to avoid him?'

'Yes. I don't think he really means it, I think it's just because of what his dad says. Like my friend Vlad – from school, like he said; if you're sexist it's because you've been brought up to think like that, you never get the chance to work it out. And I don't think Keith knows any Asians. He lives up at the Highbridge end.'

'No,' Paul said. 'In that case I don't suppose he does.'

'It's funny – *odd* – calling somebody a racist. It doesn't sound real. We have this lesson at school, Social Awareness Studies, only we call it Isms. Because that's what it is, all the time; sexism, racism, feminism. And last week we had this discussion on racism, somebody brought in a cutting from a newspaper, and everyone said how awful it was, only we've got these two girls in our class, Farida and Farzana, and nobody thought about them. They just sat there, and nobody took any notice or asked them what they thought. I mean, they never say much anyway, but that wasn't the point. Racism's just something half of us argue about while the other half do our homework. It's just a word. It doesn't mean anything because it doesn't happen to us.'

'You're all against it, of course?'

'I think most of us are.'

'So long as you don't have to do anything about it?'

'It's the first time I've had to do anything about it. Where we lived before, everyone was white anyway. If I'd met Keith there I'd never have known what he thought because he'd never have said anything. Racism was just something on the news.'

'And now it's just something that gets in the way of your homework?'

'Not to me. Not any more.'

'This is the flat,' said Paul, who had been driving with a street map propped on the steering wheel. 'I shan't be long; or do you want to come in with me?'

'I'll stay here,' Lloyd said.

'Right, we'll carry on when I get back. Sorry to run out on you, but they did say seven-thirty. We're not on double yellow lines, are we?'

Lloyd watched him run up to the front door of a tall house flanked by monkey puzzle trees. A light came on in the hall, the door opened and he went in. A few minutes later the windows on the second floor lit up. He sat in the car, fiddling with the seat belt, peering at the map in the dim light, trying to work out where he was; not far from the Riverside Sports Complex, by the look of it.

When Paul came back he was whistling.

'Perfect,' he said, folding himself down into the driving seat. 'Well, no, to be frank, it's not perfect, it needs a lot done to it, but it's just what we want. Huge front room with a north light.'

'What's that?'

'The window faces north; no direct sunlight.'

'Don't you like the sun?' Lloyd said, as they left the flat behind them.

'Sure, but not for painting. A studio should always face north. Bianca will love it.'

'Is she coming to see it?'

'At the weekend. I'll ring her tonight, but we're taking it anyway. I'll put down a deposit first thing in the morning and then, heigh-ho for a mortgage. You think a lot of Bianca, don't you?'

'Of course I do.' Lloyd thought Paul could have taken that as read.

'No "of course" about it. A lot of people loathe her.'

'Why?'

'Because she's black. That's all, no other reason, just that. They loathe her in restaurants, in trains, across the street, from the other end of town, without ever having spoken to her – like your friend Keith and his father. Look, this denying yourself the pleasure of American football because you don't know how to handle him is all very heroic, but entirely useless – a sort of futile gesture. Futile because nobody notices.'

'He notices I'm not there.'

'Yes, but he doesn't know *why* you're not there.'

'What can I tell him?'

'Not so easy.' Paul drove in silence, considering it. 'How about, "I find it very difficult to go on

seeing you because you don't like my friends,"
to which he will say, "But I don't know your
friends," and you say, "You won't like them when
you see them, but I'm not giving them up;" that
puts the ball firmly in his court.'

'How do you mean?'

'Either he'll sheer off and you can go back to
enjoying your football, or he might just make an
effort to see things from your point of view. That
may be absurdly optimistic, but it could happen,
if he values your friendship – and it sounds as if
he does. But whichever way the cookie crumbles,
at least you'll have done something – something
that *shows*; you'll have made your stand. Have
you ever heard of Pastor Niemöller?'

'Who was that?'

'Martin Niemöller, a German clergyman who
ended up in a concentration camp for opposing
the Nazis. He said: "Then they came for the Jews,
and I didn't speak up because I wasn't a Jew. And
when they came for the Catholics I didn't speak
up because I was a Protestant. Then they came
for me, and by that time there was no one left to
speak for anyone."'

When they parked the car in Sackville Street
the house was as they had left it, only the porch
light burning.

'Ingrid's still out,' Lloyd said, as they opened the
front door. 'Are you going to ring Bianca now?'

'She won't be in yet. I said I'd ring at nine,'
Paul said. 'Listen, Lloyd, I'm glad you told me, I
mean, I'm glad you told *me*. I'm flattered. But all
these friends of yours, isn't there anyone you
really talk to seriously?'

'I don't –' Lloyd began; then he remembered.
'Yes, there is.'

'Ring them, then,' Paul said, on his way upstairs. 'Spread the word.'

Lloyd hung up his jacket and went to the telephone, but as he stretched out his hand to pick up the directory, it began to ring.

Keith? No, too early. He lifted the receiver.

'Hello, Urban Blight.'

'Barbara!'

'Who were you expecting?'

'Not anyone. I was just going to make a call when you rang.'

'Thought you were quick off the mark,' Barbara said. 'Is Ingrid there?'

'No, she's gone to see a friend.'

'A bloke?'

'I don't know.'

'Bet it is,' Barbara said, 'or she'd have told you. Hope it is. I'll ring again later; do you know when she'll be back?'

'She said a couple of hours, but it's that already.'

'Ah, poor abandoned creature.'

'I've been out with Paul,' Lloyd said. 'He's found a flat – hey, Barb, don't ring at nine. He wants to call Bianca and tell her.'

'Who's Bianca?'

'His fiancée.'

'He didn't tell me her name.'

'Shouldn't think he got the chance. Probably talking about *you* all the time.'

'Belt up, Toxic Waste. We were talking about you, if you remember. You didn't like that, either. Look, the money's running out. Tell Ingrid I'll call. 'Bye.'

Lloyd hung up, wrote *YOUR DAUGHTER WILL RING* on the message pad, and opened the directory. There was only one Vladimov listed, and the address was right, so he began to dial Vlad's number.